DOC LANDED
ON A BIG DOUBLE BED,

between a man in a nightcap and a woman in a pink nightgown. Doc looked from one to the other of them. It was Rob Lynch and his wife. The Pinkerton politely raised his hat to the lady and nodded to the gentleman.

"Damn you, Weatherbee!" Lynch snarled. The tiny man had a big .45 in his bony hand. "I'm going to blow your brains out for this!"

"What! In your wife's bed?" Doc looked shocked. "Her name will be dirt."

Mrs. Lynch in her pink nightgown giggled. Or it might have been hysteria.

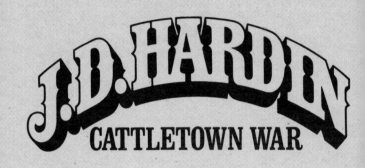

J. D. HARDIN

CATTLETOWN WAR

BERKLEY BOOKS, NEW YORK

CATTLETOWN WAR

A Berkley Book/published by arrangement with
the author

PRINTING HISTORY
Berkley edition/September 1985

ISBN: 0-425-08088-9

A BERKLEY BOOK® TM 757,375
Berkley Books are published by The Berkley Publishing Group,
200 Madison Avenue, New York, N.Y. 10016.
The name "BERKLEY" and the stylized "B" with design are trademarks
belonging to Berkley Publishing Corporation.

PRINTED IN THE UNITED STATES OF AMERICA

CHAPTER ONE

The Pinkerton operative stood in the saloon doorway and peered at the men along the bar. The hot Nevada afternoon sunshine streamed through the doorway behind him, giving the place a yellow glow from the sawdust floor to the smoke-blackened ceiling. No one was saying much. They gave the Pinkerton the usual wary glance a newcomer received, but no more than a glance. They were not impressed.

The Pinkerton saw who he was looking for—a big man in a fringed buckskin jacket that made his back look four feet wide across the shoulders. He was one of the few men in the saloon not dressed in a miner's flannel shirt and denim overalls. The man's black beard was bushy and untended, and his greasy hair hung to his shoulders. The Pinkerton needed to check on just one more thing to be sure he had his man. He saw it when the big man in the fringed jacket rolled himself a cigarette on the bar counter. The tips of all four fingers of his left hand were missing. Indians were supposed to have done it years ago. This was Ned Richmond. No doubt about it.

Richmond was one of three claim jumpers the Pinkertons had been hired to track down. The three men had forged a bill of sale and then tried to sell the claim, and other claims adjoining it, to a group of speculators. When some of the claims' real owners by chance discovered what was going on, the three men left town. In the mess they left behind them, the real owners were finding it hard to prove they still owned their claims and that the group of speculators had no valid claim on them. What the owners needed were the forged deeds and certificates, which the three had taken along with them when they skipped town.

The Pinkerton drew his .45, strode across the sawdust floor, and poked the barrel into the back of the big man in the buckskin jacket.

"You're coming with me, Ned Richmond."

Richmond didn't move a muscle. "You're wasting your time, fella. There ain't no bounty on my head."

"I'm not a bounty hunter. I'm taking you into custody for selling something that didn't belong to you down in Eureka County."

The other customers at the bar had stepped back a few paces when they saw the gun in the big man's back. It was plain horse sense to move out of the way of any stray pieces of lead that might soon be floating through the air. As the men backed along the bar, the Pinkerton operative caught a glimpse of his partner farther along it, nursing his drink and paying no mind to what was happening. He had no time to straighten out his so-called partner at this moment, but he wouldn't forget this.

"Mind if I turn around?" The big man didn't wait for permission, but slowly revolved on his heels to face the

Pinkerton, moving smoothly and steadily so as not to spook the man with the gun in his hand.

He was still turning around when his right hand pushed the Pinkerton's gun arm to one side.

The Pinkerton pulled the trigger, and the big Colt spat flame.

But Ned Richmond no longer stood before the barrel. The .45-caliber slug punctured a neat hole through a plush couch on which reclined a yellow-haired nude in a painting on the wall behind the bar.

Richmond's right hand had closed around the chambers of the Colt, preventing them from revolving and the gun from being fired again. He bent the pistol upward out of the Pinkerton's grasp and threw it across the saloon onto the sawdust floor.

"I'd kill you," he told the Pinkerton with contempt, "if it weren't for the fact I could never convince no judge it was self-defense against a little gopher like you."

He smashed his fist into the Pinkerton's mouth. The man staggered backward from the force of the blow and sat on his ass, dazed, in the sawdust.

Richmond followed through with a boot to the side of the operative's head and another to his gut as he squirmed on the floor. Then he returned to his drink with a pleased look on his face.

This was when the downed Pinkerton operative's partner finally stirred himself.

He was a big man, as tall and broad across the shoulders as Ned Richmond. His deeply tanned face sported a black mustache, and his eyes were jet black. A battered black Stetson, a scarred leather jacket, faded denims, and calfskin Middleton boots completed his outfit, except for the Remington .44 that rode easily on his right hip.

Ned Richmond's eyes narrowed as this man peeled away from the bar and ambled toward him. Richmond knew real trouble when he saw it.

"Fella there you knocked down is a friend of mine."

"Who're you?" Richmond asked.

"A friend of the fella you just knocked down."

"You got a name?"

"Raider."

"Okay, Raider, I'll tell you something. If you don't go back where you belong, you're going to be lying next to your friend on that saloon floor. That clear enough for you?"

It was clear enough for most of the customers. This time they moved off an extra-safe distance.

Raider didn't seem to understand. "Did he have your name right? Ned Richmond?"

Richmond's right hand hovered over the gun at his side, but Raider seemed relaxed and unconcerned, as if he were carrying on a friendly conversation.

"You heard my name right, mister," Richmond ground out. "Why? You got an idea of taking me into custody too?"

"Finish up your drink, Ned, and I'll buy you one for the road," Raider said with a smile. "It's the end of the trail for you—going to be a lot of years before you stand at a bar again and throw back a whiskey."

Richmond was now genuinely alarmed, yet still only half believing what he was listening to. "You going to take me in?"

"That's right."

Ned Richmond stroked his full beard with his left hand, hoping the action would distract his opponent for the split second he needed to get the better of him in a fast draw. His right hand dropped to his gun handle.

Raider wasn't fooled. His big long-barrel Remington .44

came out of its holster fast as a mule kick, and his right thumb pressed back the hammer to cock the gun before it had fully cleared leather. His forefinger was already coming down on the trigger an instant before the barrel was leveled on Ned Richmond's chest. All the movements came together at exactly the right time, before Richmond even got his revolver cocked. The Remington's hammer crashed on the firing pin, which hit the cap on the cartridge, set off the charge, and propelled the bullet forward through the barrel.

The Remington belched smoke and flame as it kicked mightily in Raider's grip. The .44-caliber lead slug caught Richmond on the breastbone. It became flattened and twisted out of shape as it plowed inward through his flesh, and its distorted form gouged a hole the size of a man's fist through his innards. The bullet tore his heart from its vessels before it lodged against his backbone.

Allan Pinkerton sat at a heavy desk in his oak-paneled office at the headquarters of the Pinkerton National Detective Agency at 191–193 Fifth Avenue in Chicago. He snorted angrily and handed a telegram to his son Robert. "Raider has killed one of the three already." His Scottish burr was made stronger by his exasperation. "We team that madman up with Orville Huggins to keep him in check and he still butchers anyone who stands in his path."

Robert finished reading the telegram and pointed out to his father, "Since Orville sent this, it's his version of events."

"Raider never sends any reports! You can't call those scrappy bits of information he occasionally sees fit to send here—you can't bestow the title 'report' on disconnected jottings like that. You'd swear he was afraid to reveal anything in case the message fell into the hands of the enemy."

Robert grinned. "I guess we're the enemy."

Allan Pinkerton fumed. "I don't train my operatives to harbor attitudes such as that. The man does what he pleases. Raider creates havoc wherever he goes. Oh, he gets the job done, I grant you that. And I'd send him on assignments no other man would survive, let alone succeed at. But I won't tolerate his anarchy. I can't afford to! He's been sent out to bring back at least one of three men so that man can be convicted. Our client must have a conviction or at least an admission of guilt to show that the mining claim was taken illegally from him. What does Raider do? Shoots him! Once there were three men. Now there are only two. Have Wagner send Raider a stiffly worded telegram explaining once again that it's the testimony or conviction of these men which is required, not their scalps."

"Yes, Father."

"Not that it will do much good. Once that man gets among vagabonds and lowlifes, he seems determined to outdo them at their own vices."

Robert tried to calm his father. "I'm sure the presence of Orville Huggins as his partner will act as a restraint on Raider."

"Orville is a fool, an incompetent!" the Scotsman stormed. "I keep him on only because of what his late father did for me. He saved my life once when I was a deputy sheriff in Dundee."

Robert had heard this story many times before and knew that the Dundee his father referred to was the suburb of Chicago and not the town in his homeland. Allan Pinkerton was in his early twenties when he and his wife took a ship from Glasgow to the New World. The ship foundered off Nova Scotia and they were lucky to reach a safe landing in a lifeboat. Thus they began their new life owning literally nothing but the wet clothes on their backs. While working as a barrel maker in Chicago, Pinkerton helped run down a gang of counterfeiters and was appointed a deputy sheriff in Dundee.

Robert spoke before his father could get launched into the story of how Orville Huggins's father had saved his life. "Orville will act as a wet blanket on whatever craziness Raider wants to get into."

"We've tried to hobble Raider before, and it's never worked," Allan Pinkerton growled.

"He's totally unpredictable," his son agreed.

"Maybe that's why he's still alive and just about one of the best damn operatives I have in the field."

Lo Sun Chang could hardly believe his eyes. He worked the sharp tip of the knife around some more in the chicken gizzard he was preparing for the meal and found a second nugget. He had expected to find the usual small pebbles that hens swallow to help them grind seeds inside the muscular walls of the gizzard. Instead he was finding gold nuggets!

Although he examined the gizzard extremely carefully, and ended by cutting it into fine slivers, he found no more nuggets. Lo Sun Chang put the knife down and thought about what he should do. There was no one he could trust. His roundeye employer would take the gold from him and say it was his, since he had bought the chicken. What of the other chickens? Twenty-three more had come in the shipment along with this one. Had they gold in their gizzards too?

No one to trust. There were three men from his part of China who worked at a mine outside the town. He would see them in a few days' time and tell them about his discovery—but only after he had killed all the other chickens for restaurant meals and searched in their gizzards. The roundeyes didn't bother with the gizzard—they threw away the whole neck of a chicken. Maybe chickens in some places always had gold nuggets in their gizzards and no one ever looked!

"Where the hell's my food?" the drunk roundeye at the restaurant shouted toward the kitchen. "You gone back to China to get it?"

Lo Sun Chang didn't like this man. Let him wait for his food, which was simmering on the stove. Lo Sun Chang had been preparing a meal for himself when he had found the nuggets. He was alone in the kitchen this evening because old Clem, the dishwasher, hadn't shown up for work yet. The restaurant wouldn't get busy for another hour or so, and there was only one early customer.

He was still standing at the chopping block with the two gold nuggets in front of him when the drunk roundeye burst through the swinging door that led into the kitchen.

Lo Sun Chang tried to hide the nuggets with his hands. He would have been successful with most men, but this roundeye was a prospector, and, in spite of being drunk, his trained eyes were quick enough to see the two pieces of pure gold.

"What you got there?" he demanded and rushed forward.

Lo Sun Chang grabbed the big knife and kept him at a distance.

The prospector ignored the blade. He swayed on his feet and stared at the cut-up chicken neck and one of the nuggets not quite covered by the Chinese man's left hand. Then he rushed out the back door of the kitchen into the yard behind the building. Lo Sun Chang heard the cackling and squawking from the henhouse. Moments later the prospector came back in the door with a protesting chicken held by the neck in each hand.

He put one of the birds under his arm to free both hands to grapple with the second. He stretched the neck of the flapping fowl on the chopping block before the Chinese cook, who stood there motionless with the knife still in his right hand. Then Lo Sun Chang whacked down the blade on the chicken's neck, severing its head. A quick cut into the gizzard revealed a rounded lump of solid gold.

The prospector grinned at the cook and reached for the next chicken.

Orville Huggins looked at Raider severely across the breakfast table in the hotel dining room. "I think there's no call for you to say the unkind things you've been saying to me."

Raider had a hangover, and Orville's voice was like metal scraping on metal. "I've forgotten what I called you. Tell me, so I can call you those names again."

"I don't think it's fitting and respectable for a Pinkerton operative to wallow in whiskey and consort with soiled doves," Orville pronounced. "When I tried to insist on your returning to your hotel last night, it was to protect the reputation of the Pinkerton National Detective Agency. I have it on good authority that Mr. Allan Pinkerton himself personally selected me for this task."

Raider tried shouting—but his head hurt too much. He glowered at Orville instead.

"You may not remember that you struck me," Orville complained. "And when I tried to defend myself, they threw me out for fighting instead of you!"

Raider smiled. "I was buying drinks. You were interfering."

"No one in this town has any morals."

"Except you, Orville," Raider said wearily. "And you have enough to provide for us all."

When Raider arrived in the dining room, Huggins was halfway through a solid breakfast of steak and eggs. The waiter finally arrived to take Raider's order.

"Two beers."

Huggins looked up in surprise. "Raider, I don't want a beer at this hour of the morning."

"Both of them are for me," Raider snarled.

The waiter smirked and went to get them.

"This is what I mean," Orville said earnestly. "You're lowering the good name of the Pinkertons by this kind of behavior."

After breakfast they went together to the Western Union office to see if there was anything from Chicago. There was. Huggins read the telegram first, then handed the sheet of paper in the clerk's copperplate handwriting to Raider.

A major error was committed in the loss of one suspect out of three. Such gross stupidity must be prevented from recurring. Disciplinary measures are under consideration.

Wagner

Raider calmly handed the telegram back to Orville Huggins. He said, with a relaxed smile, "This, of course, is based on whatever report you saw fit to send them."

"I suppose so," Orville said, furtively avoiding his eyes.

"Way I saw what happened was you and me traced Ned Richmond here to North Fork after finding that he'd blown all his money in Virginia City. I guessed he was looking for either one or both of his partners, knowing somehow they are in this part of Nevada. Now that his money was gone, he could pressure them into giving him more. I said we weren't going to get a thing from Richmond—he wasn't the kind to talk, no matter what. We had to rely on him leading us to the others. That was when you pulled your stunt, sticking a gun in his back and getting yourself stomped."

"I didn't know you would be in the bar, Raider. I thought arresting him was the right thing to do."

"Bullshit! You're telling the truth when you say you didn't know I'd be in the bar. You thought you was making a big arrest on your own to earn your big marks back in Chicago. Instead, you gave the game away to Richmond, who knew then he had been cottoned onto. I had no choice but to try to take him in before he could warn the others. Like I foresaw, he went down fighting rather than give in. You put any of that in your report?"

"I stated the facts as I saw them," Orville said defensively. "And I think they're going to buy my version of things rather than yours."

Raider smiled again. "You know, Orville, I think for once you may be right. It seems to me that if you're the kind of operative that Allan Pinkerton wants, he should get what he deserves. I quit."

Orville panicked. "Oh no, Raider, you can't do that!"

"Sure I can." Raider shook him by the hand. "Orville, I want to wish you all the luck in the world."

Raider left Orville Huggins in the middle of North Fork's only street. Orville suddenly felt very much alone.

"You the Pinkerton who shot Ned Richmond?" the barkeep at the East Run saloon asked.

"I ain't a Pinkerton no more," Raider muttered.

"How come?"

"'Cause I found something better to do. Go 'way and bother someone else."

The barkeep didn't move. "There's some who's looking to hire fast guns in these parts. They pay real good, too.

From what I hear about the way you got the drop on Ned Richmond, you'd make a bundle. If you want me to, I'll mention it to these parties that you been in here."

"You always talk your customers to death?" Raider growled.

The barkeep laughed and moved down the counter. Raider had only a moment of peace before a stocky little man with a jaunty air and a rascally look on his face stood next to him. Raider paid no attention to him until the man poked him in the ribs and pointed to a dirty red bandanna he had placed on the counter before him. The man lifted a fold of the bandanna and revealed about twenty small gold nuggets.

Raider had seen bigger nuggets and more of them, and he was in no mood to listen to some miner's long tale about his luck with a shovel and pan in some stream gravel. "I seen better."

"Not from a hen's craw, you haven't. Mind you, these ain't all from one hen. Near twenty-five birds. This is half of what I found. I had to give the other half to a fella who happened to be there so he would keep his mouth closed. Don't want word to spread about this—least not till after I find the gravel in which those chickens was picking."

Raider was hooked. He poured the man a whiskey from his bottle and listened to his story. There was no Chinese cook in this version. The man was a prospector and miner, his name was Jedediah Budd, and he'd found the gold in the chicken's gizzard when he demanded that part of the bird with his meal.

"They told me to go cook it myself. They weren't going to do it for me. So I did. And found the gold. I took the rest of that shipment of chickens and slaughtered them all, one after the other, right there in that kitchen—till there was feathers and blood and dead hens all over the place. That's when the owner of the restaurant came in, made me pay for them, and told me not to come back. I had to buy the silence of one of the kitchen help with half the gold."

Raider laughed. "Now that sure is one of the tallest tales I ever did hear."

"You're thinking I'm trying to put over a fast one?" Budd said. "Well, listen here, Mr. Raider, I'm making you an offer the like of which you won't get again."

"I got no money to invest."

Budd nodded. "I know the lousy pay you Pinkertons collect. This won't cost you a penny. I heard you say a while back that you quit the Pinkertons. You're just what I need. A trained detective. I bet you can track those chickens down."

Raider looked amazed. "Why don't you just ask the restaurant owner where he bought them?"

"Well, he's kind of mad at me for killing all of them. He thinks I'm some kind of loco who gets his fun from cutting off chicken heads. He told me sure as hell he'd kill me stone dead if I ever came near him again. This morning when I saw him on the street, I ran and hid round the corner of a building. But now if you was to go in that restaurant and start up a conversation with him about the madman who killed all his chickens and kind of casually ask him where the shipment of those birds came from..."

"You're really serious?" Raider asked.

Jedediah Budd pointed to the nuggets in the bandanna. "You just think of those laying around so plentiful in the gravel that goddamn fool hens swallow them because they think they're stones. A thought like that is enough to make any man serious. And especially a man who has just quit his job and don't want to work as a hired gun. Least of all, that's what I thought I heard you saying to the barkeep."

"What do I get for finding where the hens came from?" Raider asked.

"It ain't going to work as smooth as that. When you find out where he bought them, you got to come with me, then we both pick over the gravel, and we take the gold we find to the assayer. We split the money half and half. So you see, you got nothing to lose except a few days while we find the place."

While Raider was pouring himself a drink and thinking about it, a thin-faced man with red-rimmed eyes came up to the bar and stared hungrily at the gold nuggets scattered in the bandanna.

"These yours?" he asked Budd.

"Yep," Budd snapped, but he was small in size, and his voice didn't have a fighting edge to it.

"They're mine now." The man stretched out his left hand and grabbed a fistful of nuggets. His gun hand stayed down close to his hip.

"Raider!" Jedediah squawked. "This fella is robbing me of my gold!"

Raider shook his head wonderingly. "I always heard the sight of gold drives some men crazy. Now I'm seeing it with my own eyes." He sipped some whiskey, holding the glass in his left hand while his gun hand drifted casually near the handle of his Remington. "Tell me, stranger," he said in a friendly way to the thin-faced man, "are you having some kind of brainstorm that you think you can walk up and grab another man's gold?"

The man's left fist tightened on the nuggets. "I don't see no one here who can stop me."

"You must have trouble with your eyesight, then." Raider was filling his and Jedediah's glasses from the bottle. He slammed the whiskey bottle down hard on the man's knuckles.

The stranger howled, dropped the gold, and held his hurting hand with the other. He backed off, and trouble-makers down the bar laughed loudly at him to let him know that they'd seen him bested without a shot fired.

This riled the thin-faced man so that he forgot about the pain in his left hand. "I'm going to walk out this here door," he yelled at Raider, "and I expect you to be coming along after me. We going to settle this thing out there in the street."

"You're going to be a while waiting for me," Raider told him nonchalantly. "I'm a slow drinker, and I'm comfortable here."

The stranger went through the door, and everyone in the saloon figured that was that. After a few jokes at his expense, they soon forgot about him.

Then they heard shouts from outside. He was yelling for Raider to come out.

"I'm still waiting for you!"

Raider ignored this and went on talking with Jedediah Budd.

Then a bullet shattered the saloon's front window and whizzed over Raider's head.

He looked out through the window frame, which still held some long slivers of glass. The thin-faced man was grinning in at him as he stood in the middle of the street and replaced the spent shell in his revolver.

Raider straightened up to his full height. "There are some things no man can be expected to take."

"Blow his ass away, Raider," Jedediah cackled. "It's only self-defense, sure as God's in heaven."

Raider came out the door, pulling down the brim of his black Stetson to shield his eyes from the bright sunlight. The other man's shooting iron was back in the holster on his right hip. He was twenty yards away. Raider reckoned he'd be in a hurry, to take whatever advantage he could of the sunlight's dazzling effect on the newly emerged man's eyes.

Sure enough, the thin-faced man went for his gun without delay. Even though Raider guessed he would do so, he was faster on the draw than the big ex-Pinkerton expected.

Without waiting to take aim, he knocked off two shots before Raider got one off. Each of the bullets missed Raider by more than a yard and hummed harmlessly down the middle of the almost empty street.

No man knew better than Raider that it was a waste of time to aim a revolver as carefully as he would a rifle, because of the sidearm's much shorter barrel and more powerful kick. But Raider knew that a bullet fired wild was a bullet wasted. Both he and every skilled gunfighter he knew sacrificed that tiny fraction of time needed to take rapid aim before pulling the trigger. Sometimes the delay could cost a man his life, but much more often it meant the difference between hitting and missing. In fact, most agreed that the quickness and deadliness of a gunfighter's eye were as important as those of his hand.

The Remington .44 cracked once in the dry Nevada air. The lead slug tore off most of the man's thin face. The gun dropped from his hand before he could get off a third shot. He flopped on his back onto the red dust of the street. One leg twitched, and his right hand opened and closed. That was all.

Drinks in hand, the jokers from the saloon came outside to take a look. They screwed up their faces at the sight and hurried back inside.

Raider waited for the marshal. Like Jedediah Budd had said, it was only self-defense. Even if it was the second time in a matter of days.

CHAPTER TWO

"I'm too tattered-looking and too stupid to talk with them," Jedediah Budd claimed. "Settled farming folk like them would be more likely to shoot at me than talk to me about chickens."

Raider had to grant him that he had a point there. "What about me?" he asked. "Do I look the sort you would believe was interested in poultry?"

Jedediah looked him over. "Sure you do."

Raider started indignantly, then saw that Budd was joking him.

"You got no trouble," Jedediah went on. "You still got your Pinkerton identification papers with you? Good. Well, you go up to the house and keep them talking while I take a look at the soil. I can tell pay dirt in four seconds flat— but give me ten minutes to check the place thoroughly."

Raider nodded, and they rode together toward the farmhouse.

They had ridden south from North Fork after Raider was told by the restaurant owner where the chickens came from. The first contact proved to be a dead loss. He was only a middleman who traded in hens but raised none himself. But he remembered a shipment of fifty Rhode Island Reds, half of which he sold to the restaurant owner. He'd be pleased to help the Pinkertons, he told Raider, only he didn't want to cause trouble for nobody. Raider told him he was a real nice guy to think of that but that he had to think of himself too—and the only surefire way for him to stay out of trouble himself was to tell what he knew. Raider had been directed to this isolated farm in a lonely valley.

"I don't see no chickens," Raider said as he rode toward the house.

But Jedediah had already dismounted and was too busy checking the ground for nuggets to hear what he said.

Raider was still fifty yards from the front door of the farmhouse when a rifle barrel poked through an open window.

"Rein in your horse, mister, and stop right where you are." It was a woman's voice, and she sounded like she meant what she said. After Raider had complied with her request, she called to him, "Stay back where you are and state your business. And be quick about it."

"Calm yourself, woman," Raider said in what he hoped was a soothing voice. It was not a good feeling to have an unseen nervous woman peering along the sights of a rifle at him. And no matter how shaky her aim, she could hardly miss from this distance. "I'm asking about a shipment of fifty Rhode Island Reds you sold a few days ago. Were they raised on this farm?"

"Ain't no chickens raised on this farm. Who's that fella poking around out in the dirt back there?"

Raider decided to take a chance. "That man is a gov'ment

inspector, ma'am." There was a long pause before he added, "I'm just along to see he don't come to no harm."

Finally she called out, "We don't want no gov'ment people hereabouts. If my husband was home, he'd run that fella right off his land."

"Lot of folks feel that way, ma'am," Raider said sympathetically. "Where'd you say those Rhode Island Reds came from?"

"Ain't no chickens raised here. I told you that. Once on a time we used to raise all kinds of animals here, but now those miners are so hungry and pay such big prices, we can hardly keep nothing on the land for more than a few days before it's bought off us, no matter how scrawny it is. You hold right where you are, mister, and I'll look it up in the books. I'll have you know I trained as a bookkeeper, and I keep business records for everything. It helps pass the time out here. Don't you come no nearer this house, though, because I'm watching you all the time."

The rifle barrel was withdrawn, and in a minute Raider was directed to another farm in another valley.

Raider raised his hat to the open window. "Thank you, ma'am." He had never caught sight of her, but at least she had not drawn a bead on him again with the rifle.

Her voice called after him, "Don't forget to take that gov'ment critter along with you."

Lo Sun Chang and three men from his hometown in China followed Raider and Jedediah Budd at a distance. In fact, they hung so far back that they lost them on several occasions. But since neither of the two roundeyes seemed in much of a hurry, they had been able to search this way and that in order to locate them again.

"They must not see us," Lo Sun Chang warned the others in their native dialect. None spoke much English.

One had remembered seeing Raider up close in town the time he killed Ned Richmond. He snapped his fingers four times. "He would kill all of us like that. Four bullets. He would not miss with even one."

The others looked impressed.

Lo Sun Chang explained, "The prospector Budd hired this gunman to kill me if I try to claim my half share of the gold when it is found. Since we Chinese cannot become citizens and cannot own land in America, Budd sees no reason why he should honor his agreement with me. He is the sort who would cheat any man—only it is a lot easier if the man is Chinese. We must stay far back or this white devil Raider will surely destroy us with his lightning gun."

When Raider and Budd had left the house with the lone woman and her rifle, the four Chinese had approached her. Her first shot was several feet above their heads. Her second, several inches. They turned their horses about and galloped away. Then two of them crawled on their bellies through the tall grass till they got near the house again. They found no sign of nuggets. The woman spotted the two men just as they were leaving and speeded them on their way with bullets from her repeating rifle.

"We have a big problem here," Lo Sun Chang told the others. "Budd can talk with these people, yet they will not talk with us. First we get kicked, and now we got shot at."

It was true that the wholesaler whom Raider and Budd had first approached actually physically kicked two of the Chinese out of his office. He had assumed they were looking for work, and when he told them he had none for them and they didn't leave immediately, trying instead to say things to him in their bad English, he booted them out. The four Chinese had been too far away to see that the lone woman had held Raider off with her rifle. They assumed she had spoken with him in a friendly way and turned her gun on them simply because they were Chinese.

Lo Sun Chang had the answer: "We must not try to speak with the demons. We must follow and watch. When Budd finds the gold, then we will strike."

"Darnedest thing," Raider said to Jedediah Budd as they rode across a valley. "We got four Chinamen on our tail."

"Four?"

Raider glanced at him. "You seem more surprised at the number than the fact they're Chinamen or that we're being followed in the first place."

"Any man who's looked for gold is used to human vultures and human coyotes sniffing around him," Budd said. "It goes with the territory."

"Guess so. But why Chinamen?"

"That fella I had to pay off in the kitchen to keep his mouth shut was a Chinaman. Remember I told you I had to give him half the nuggets so he wouldn't tell the restaurant owner? I bet it's him and some of his cronies skulking back there, hoping to rob us. Though I ain't seen no one, and I been keeping a wary eye out. You sure they been tailing us?"

Raider nodded and said nothing more.

The way out of the valley into the next one was through a narrow pass cut by a stream through a spine of low hills. Aspen and willows sheltered the stream banks, and a clear trail was worn in the lush grass.

"You go on ahead," Raider told Budd. "Take it easy so they'll be sure to catch glimpses of you through the trees."

Budd hesitated, then decided to say nothing. He had already learned that when Raider meant business he used words sparingly and wanted none in reply. Budd knew he had to do what he was told in these circumstances or he would damn soon find himself on his own. The last thing he wanted was for Raider to talk to the goddamn Chinaman and find out Budd had promised him a half share in the gold. With half promised to the Chinaman and the other to the one-time Pinkerton, he had nothing left for himself. Instead of cheating both of them out of their shares, as he intended, if these two came together Jedediah Budd could be the one who would end up with nothing! But now he felt his best bet was to go along with what Raider wanted and hope for the best.

Raider watched him wend his way on horseback through the trees in the narrow pass. The scrub-covered hills rose steeply to form the sides of the pass. Raider tied his horse to an aspen in full sight of the trail. He stayed with the horse, his hand patting its forehead and nostrils, ready to stop it from neighing to approaching horses. The four Chinese would expect nothing till they had rounded a bend in the trail and found themselves face to face with him. Raider loosened his big Remington six-shooter in its holster, relaxed his body, and waited.

It was more than ten minutes before his horse's ears twitched forward. The animal looked downtrail and tried to shake its head free of Raider's hand.

The four Chinese came round the bend in the trail one behind the other. At first they didn't even recognize Raider, thinking he was someone else who just happened to be there. Then when Raider stood in the trail, blocking their way, they glanced quickly at one another, anxiety spreading across their faces. None of them were armed. Raider did not draw his gun.

"What do you want from me?" the big man with the black mustache asked, catching their lead horse by the reins.

The lead Chinese dismounted, then the other three. They were dressed in loose blue tunics and pants, wore nothing on their feet but sandals, and had their long hair woven into a pigtail behind their heads. They came together and looked at him but said nothing, neither to him nor to each other.

Raider figured he had frightened them. "I ain't going to kill you. But you ain't leaving here in one piece lest I know what you came here for in the first place. I ain't gonna have people on my coattails without I know why they're there." He pointed at one of the four. "You! Why're you following me?"

The man gazed back at him in silence, with no expression on his face.

This made Raider kind of mad. "You speak any English? I know that you understand me. It's no use you pretending not to."

The man stared back at him without even blinking.

Raider wished silently to himself that all four of them had guns so he could blast the shit out of them, instead of all this peaceful palavering. His own private code didn't allow him to pull a gun on an unarmed man—not even four unarmed men. Each of them weighed about half what he did and were hardly chest-high to him. Heck, Raider thought, this was almost like arguing with women.

"You understand me okay," Raider said to the same man. "I want to hear why you been dogging me all this way."

He strode up to the man and stood a few inches from him, looming over him and intending to put a scare into him.

The Chinese man never moved a muscle and stared ahead into one of Raider's shirt buttons.

Raider poked his finger in the man's chest—then suddenly felt himself rising from the ground as if he weighed no more than a feather, turn some kind of somersault in midair, then crash heavily on his ass in the dust.

The four Chinese stood there looking at him. They weren't even laughing at him. Nothing showed on their faces.

Raider grinned, feeling foolish. "Hell, I've had that done to me before. I don't know how you do it, but it didn't stop me then, and it ain't going to stop me now."

He got to his feet and brushed some dust off his denims. Then he went right back to the man who had thrown him.

This time he was going to watch every move. The little bastard was not going to take him by surprise with his quickness. Raider grabbed the man by his upper arms, meaning to lift him up off his feet and look him level in the eyes. Only things didn't work out that way.

The varmint wriggled out of his clutches fast as an eel, gave him a small push against one hip that threw him off balance for a moment, and whipped him into the air again, like he weighed no more than an aspen leaf. Except a leaf lands gently, and Raider came down heavily on his ass. His right hand automatically brushed against his Remington to make sure it still sat in its holster.

Raider jumped to his feet. He spoke to the man who threw him. "All right, you've had your fun and games with me. Next time we play it my way, not yours. I'll tell you what that means. It means a pine box. One for each of you, if I find enough cash on your bodies to pay for them. Now get on them horses and go your way while I go mine. Or else talk."

The four men went obediently to their horses, climbed into the saddle, and silently went back the way they had come.

Raider caught up with Jedediah Budd in a little while.

"I didn't hear no shooting," Budd said. "You deal with them?"

"Sure," Raider said shortly.

Budd looked mighty worried. After they had ridden for a spell and were coming into the next valley, he said, "Raider,

I thought I caught a movement behind us, back a ways. Them Chinamen still tailing us?"

Raider nodded.

"How come you didn't gun down the little bastards?"

Raider shrugged. "They're harmless."

The rancher and what looked to be his son rode out to meet Raider and Jedediah Budd before they reached the house. Raider asked if they had recently sold a shipment of fifty Rhode Island Reds.

"You're talking about hens?" the rancher asked, amazed.

"I am."

"Does this look to you like a poultry farm? Me, I'm a cattleman, and I'm proud of it. We don't have no hens around here except for the few you see yonder by the ranch-house door. And they ain't Rhode Island Reds neither."

"They're Wyandottes," his son put in.

"Whatever they are, they lay eggs for us, and they're not for sale. If you want steers, we got good beef here. But no sheep. No pigs. No hens. Nothing like that. This is a cattle ranch, mister."

"Guess we made a mistake," Raider allowed. "Good day to you."

As Raider and Jedediah rode off, the rancher's son asked his father, "Why did you lie to them? Those were the hens we reared. We got nothing to hide. Have we?"

"Who knows? I didn't like the looks of those two. 'Specially not the big one with the black hat and mustache and easy-riding gun. When a man like that asks a question and you don't know why he's asking, you don't give him a true answer. For all we know, some pard of theirs choked to death on a bone from one of those hens and they've come to revenge themselves on us. There's mighty crazy critters on the loose out there. You don't never let a badman come to rest easy in your nearabouts. You say or do whatever you have to so you can prod him to move on. Whatever those two were after, it sure as hell wasn't chickens."

"We got no work here," the rancher shouted at the four Chinese.

He had ridden over to find out what they were doing in a dry wash not far from his ranch house. He was even a little alarmed, because these four plus the other two totaled six strangers in a single day, on a ranch where he often went months on end without having even a lone drifter pass by. These Chinese were unarmed, and they smiled and bowed to him.

Lo Sun Chang pointed around at the locoweed. "We pick before flowers come and seed is spread. We pick all day and you feed us one meal."

It so happened that in the last year the rancher had lost a good horse and a dozen cattle because of the locoweed along this wash.

"All right," he said. "You come by the ranch house at sundown and we'll feed you. You can stay the night in the bunkhouse."

"Leastways we seem to have lost them damn Chinamen," Jedediah Budd said to Raider with a look back over his shoulder.

"I think they got more sense than either of us," Raider muttered as he rode easily along. "Excepting it's hens, this is what's called a wild goose chase."

"That woman steered us wrong. We gotta go back and talk with her again."

Raider shook his head. "No, Jed. This ain't my kind of work. I wish you the best of luck, and I give up any claim on the gold if you find it. I've had enough. I'm going back to North Fork."

Budd complained, whined, and persuaded all the way, but he couldn't change Raider's mind. However, Budd himself showed no urge to go on alone, and he accompanied Raider back to North Fork. Before they reached the town, he was already telling Raider about a promising claim he owned a day's ride west of the town. He offered Raider a partnership in it in exchange for work with a pick and shovel. Raider said he'd think about it.

Orville Huggins was one of the first men they saw when they hit North Fork. Although he was limping down the town street, he broke into a hobbling run when he caught sight of Raider.

"You come back! You come back!"

"Go to hell, Huggins," Raider growled. "I told you once and I'll tell you again—if Allan Pinkerton thinks you're a better operative than me, I don't belong to such an organization. Go take your troubles elsewhere."

"Raider, listen to me—"

"Huggins, only time you and me is going to meet up with each other is when I got a price on my head and the Pinkertons send you out to bring me in. You think you could take me?"

Orville got such a nervous look on his face at the thought of this that both Budd and Raider had to laugh.

"Raider, you gotta hear this," Orville pleaded. "After you took off, I realized I'd done something stupid, and I was afraid to tell them in Chicago that I had been the cause of you quitting the Pinkertons. They'd have booted me out of the agency for sure. As it is, only the old man insists on keeping me because my father once helped him. It's a great story. Once . . ."

"Hang on a moment, Orville," Raider interrupted. "Are

you telling me that you've been sending in reports without mentioning I quit?"

"I wasn't sure how to phrase it without making it look like my fault," Orville said.

"Huggins, you're an even bigger asshole than I suspected. So I'm still a Pinkerton. How about that." Raider thought that over. "I'm still a Pinkerton. Come on, Huggins, I'll buy you a drink. This here is Jedediah Budd, and we been out working up a thirst among the chicken farmers."

"That sounds like a good steady occupation," Orville said as Raider and Budd tied their horses to the rail outside the Golden Opportunity saloon.

"I hear chicken farming has a whole new future in agriculture. Is that what you were considering, Raider?"

"Don't mind Orville," Raider explained to Budd. He appeared to notice his fellow operative's limp for the first time. "What's wrong? You got a nail in your boot?"

"No. A bullet in the ass."

Raider knew by the ashamed look on his face that this was no attempt at a wisecrack.

"Who shot you?"

"I was catching up with Eddie Buckley when a small claim holder named Boyle shot me by mistake with a small-caliber derringer. It's not so bad."

Eddie Buckley was one of the three claim jumpers they had been looking for. Ned Richmond was the dead one, and Dan Harewood the third. So Orville had made contact—if that was the way to put it—while Raider had been gone and, unless Raider was way off beam, had made a mess of it.

"You make a mess of it, Orville?"

Huggins nodded.

Raider said, "Let's get that whiskey."

The Golden Opportunity didn't have much to recommend it in the way of saloons, with a canvas roof over four log walls and a dirt floor. Liquor was served on a counter of planks supported by beer kegs.

Raider poured each of them a glass from a bottle with a Kentucky bourbon label. He tasted his drink, grimaced, and said, "I guess when they finish the bourbon, they refill the bottle with local spirits. Tell me what you did to get shot, Orville."

"I tried to take Buckley alive, Raider."

"Is he dead?"

"No, he's just fine, from what I hear," Orville said. "He's made a big joke of the whole thing. In fact, I was kind of worried some of the things Buckley's been saying about Pinkertons might get back to Chicago. Which was why I was sure glad to see you, Raider, when you showed up like you just did."

Raider just nodded and poured himself another drink. "You know where to find Buckley?"

"Sure. He and Dan Harewood have bought themselves a claim out by Blood Iron Creek."

Jedediah Budd came alive. "That's out by my claim, Raider, the one I was going to cut you in on."

"There's something new, Raider," Orville said with a meaningful look toward Budd. "There's a reward out of three hundred dollars a head for anyone who directly assists in the apprehension of those two. It can't be claimed by us Pinkertons, of course."

Jedediah's eyes lit up. "Six hundred for the two! I'll cut each of you in for kickbacks of twenty-five dollars apiece. That's fifty bucks each for the two. I just go along with you while you both grab them, and afterward I claim the reward for taking you there. You can't do better than that."

Raider shook his head. "Jed, I've nothing against you getting the reward, but you have to keep the whole thing with no kickbacks to us."

"If you insist," Budd agreed happily.

"One other thing," Raider added. "Dealing with me, you're going to have to earn that reward."

"I was afraid of that," Budd said.

After the four Chinese had spent a third full day of backbreaking work on the dry wash, the rancher said to his family, "I never seen workers like them in my life before—they go all day with a quart of water and nothing to eat till we feed them at sundown."

His son shook his head. "I dunno. It looks funny to me. They spend more time scratching in the dirt than they do pulling up locoweed. When I asked one of them, he said it was important to get the plants out by the roots. Them Chinamen is strange folk all right."

"Let them be," his father counseled. "They got their ways, we got ours. So long as they tear up a lot of weed and don't eat much of our food, we got the best of the bargain." He smiled. "You hear them out there in the bunkhouse, jabbering on in that talk of theirs?"

The voices of the four Chinese men had grown loud on the still evening air as their discussion in their native tongue grew more intense—whether they should return to China and buy land with their gold or send money to bring their families to America.

CHAPTER THREE

When a prospector makes a strike, he must place a location or discovery monument at the point where he made the strike. The commonest discovery monument is a wood stake surrounded by a pile of stones or earth. As part of the discovery monument, he puts a notice of location in a tin can to protect it from the elements. This piece of paper gives the position of the strike, saying exactly how far away it is from some easily recognized fixed object in the terrain, and also the date and name of the claim, and the name of its discoverer and those of any witnesses.

After doing this the prospector has twenty days to stake out his claim. He cannot claim more than fifteen hundred feet along a vein or lode, and the greatest width can be no more than six hundred feet, three hundred to each side of the strike. A placer claim—in gravels rather than solid rock—differs from a lode claim in that it can be either a square or rectangle and cover as much as twenty acres.

There is nothing to stop partners in a venture from staking side-by-side claims, one each for any number of partners.

When the claim has been staked, the prospector has ninety days to sink a location or discovery shaft measuring four feet by six by ten, or an open cut or trench of equivalent area, and to record a certificate of location.

The law is clear on one point. For a man to hold his claim, he has to perform a fixed amount of labor or improvements, called assessment work, on the claim every year. So long as he does the required annual assessment of work, the claim remains his indefinitely. If for some reason he abandons his claim by not doing the assessment of work, the claim falls open to anyone who wants it.

While the holder of a valuable claim can sell it easily, the owners of unpromising ones often simply abandon them when they can't find buyers.

Eddie Buckley and Dan Harewood had their own system. They liked to buy a claim of proven worth and then buy out cheap all the neighboring claim holders. If they couldn't be bought out cheap, they were driven off. When Buckley and Harewood had enough adjoining claims to put together a big parcel of land, they sold it to eastern speculators at prime prices, using as a bait the certified assays of the original pay-dirt claim they had bought. Since some of their parcels of mining properties had actually paid off handsomely to the speculators, Buckley and Harewood found themselves to be big names. Now that Richmond was no longer around, it meant all the more for themselves.

When the three first started out, they had paid roughnecks to keep claim holders from doing their annual assessment work and then jumped their claims after the year was up. But in a while they reckoned this took too long, and they speeded up the process any way they could. They had some shootings, and these brought the sheriff and some risk while lawmen were poking about. A beating with a two-by-four was often more effective than a bullet.

It was Dan Harewood who came up with one of the best solutions—a man with a broken leg couldn't work, couldn't follow them around to cause trouble, and was usually damn glad to accept any cash at all he could lay his hands on. So they broke legs. Usually not out by the claim, and none of the three would ever be personally involved. Just a fight outside a saloon or in a dark alley, and a boot down on the thigh or shin of the fallen man. It took months to heal. Some never walked right again. They all gave up their claims.

But some counterfeited certificates and a bribe to the recording clerk were a quicker and cleaner way of doing business. Dates could be erased and substituted, signatures could be expertly copied—and a claim holder, absent from his workings for a few months, could return to find he had "sold out," according to official documents, and that others mining there now were doing so legally.

"That dumb bastard Boyle is dug into his hole like a badger, and he won't move, no matter what," Eddie Buckley told Dan Harewood. "We got this whole parcel ready for sale except for that one claim plumb in the middle of it."

"You think he killed Crowe?"

"I'm sure of it," Eddie replied. "Night before last I told Crowe to smash him up real good, and next morning Crowe is found on the side of the trail between here and North Fork with his head stove in and a bloodstained stone beside him. I'd told Crowe not to shoot him—not to make it look like a hired killing, but more like a miner's fight or an accident. You wanted that. I guess Crowe underestimated him."

Dan Harewood nodded. "He wasn't the first gunslinger to think he could handle a miner real easy and found out the hard way that he couldn't."

"So what are we going to do with Boyle? He won't sell out. He won't scare. If only that fool Pinkerton Huggins had been willing to lodge charges against him for shooting him."

Harewood laughed. "Those charges wouldn't have stuck. Boyle had every right to shoot Huggins in the ass for trespassing on his property. The pity is he didn't kill Huggins. Boyle might have found that killing a Pinkerton would've..." His voice trailed off and he looked at Buckley. "Eddie, are you thinking what I'm thinking?"

Buckley lit a cheroot and spat. "Let's do it."

Jedediah Budd knew the old saying that miners are worse than women for peeking at one another out of the corner of the eye to see how well got up the others are. Only they're not looking at each other's clothes but the quality of the other man's ore—always watching for what they call jewelry ore, which is high in color and in metal content. Jedediah knew that his return to his unworked claim and his labors there, in the midst of other previously unproductive and now deserted claims, would soon attract attention. He kept to himself for the most part, and when anyone was around, he put on a show of high spirits and let them see he was well pleased with his results without saying so.

Dan Harewood and Eddie Buckley rode by after a couple of days. They threw a practiced eye over the workings.

"What's all the flurry here?" Harewood asked without dismounting. "I hear tell you're working up a storm out here, and now that we come to see what's up, I don't see nothing. You hardly even made a scrape along that drift yet. This is no more than a coyote hole. What do you expect to find?"

"Silver," Jedediah said.

Harewood laughed. "You married to this prospect?"

This was mining jargon for steadily working a claim in spite of a lack of reward.

"Hell, no," Budd said. "I wish I was back in Slick Rock, Colorado. I should never have left."

Harewood and Buckley exchanged a wary glance.

"What's keeping you on here?" Buckley asked. "And don't tell me it's silver, cause it ain't. All you're going to get from this digging is copper and lead, and that ain't worth shit unless they build a spur from the railroad up here. That may be sometime in the next century."

"If ever," Harewood added.

This was true, as Budd well knew. The claim, as it stood, was worthless. Gold or silver was easily recovered from its crushed ore, and with fairly simple equipment. Its bulk was small, so it was no problem to ship by mule. Copper ore produced ten to twenty pounds per ton (high-grade gold ore produced only two to five ounces of pure gold), but the copper had low value, its smelting required much equipment, and the copper matte was costly to transport. Buckley and Harewood were shrewd. They still hadn't heard why Budd was working this claim, and obviously they considered it their business to find out. Which was just what Budd wanted. He knew he had come on too strong with what he said about Slick Rock. Now he talked on with them, so they could see he wasn't crazy and could guess he was hiding something from them.

Budd spent a while telling them a story about Mormons a few years back in Las Vegas, in the southern part of the state. "These Mormons regarded themselves as pioneers and homesteaders and condemned those they claimed were skimming the cream off the country with a six-shooter and a whiskey bottle. Anyway, they soon found themselves in need of bullets. Now, you know you never see Mormons digging for gold—instead they's always planting corn and stuff. But this lot had to dig for lead so they could smelt it and cast the metal in bullet molds. The lead was too hard for them to smelt, so they gave up. A few years later some good old boys found out what was wrong with that 'lead.' Hell, it was half silver—that's why it wouldn't melt down easy."

Neither Harewood nor Buckley said a word.

Budd looked offended. "What's the matter? You don't believe my story?"

"We know it's true," Harewood said. "We heard it before."

They rode away, clearly unsatisfied with their visit.

That night Budd went to a tent saloon on the mine fields. He had himself a lot of whiskey, and several men saw him grinning drunkenly at gold nuggets tied in a bandanna. Budd could handle his liquor better than he was pretending, and it was known that he could handle a gun if the need arose. He got back to the shack at his claim safe enough.

Next morning he didn't have long to wait. He crawled out of the shack when he heard horses' hooves, blinked his eyes in the light, and ran his fingers through his hair.

"Either of you gents happen to have a drink along with you?" he asked.

Buckley took a whiskey bottle from the side pocket of the greatcoat he was wearing to keep out the morning chill. Budd shivered and took a long toke on the bottle. He coughed till tears came to his eyes and handed the bottle back to the man in the saddle.

Harewood was staring at a patch of gravel and alluvial soil dumped over three adjoining claims by some long-vanished stream. A slow smile began to spread across his face.

"You didn't find those nuggets along a vein in hard rock,"

he said. "I been hearing how they look. Where did you find them?"

"In the gizzards of chickens," Budd said truthfully.

Harewood and Buckley laughed.

Harewood went on. "Now, if I was to look for nuggets out here, I'd try that gravel and alluvial soil over there. Pity none of it is on your claim, Budd."

Eddie Buckley seemed shocked. "Mr. Harewood, surely you ain't claiming Mr. Budd is sneaking out on his neighbors' claims and picking them over like a common thief."

"The thought had occurred to me," Harewood confessed mockingly.

Buckley turned to look at Jedediah. "Why, they hang people for that in these parts, so I hear tell."

Harewood and Buckley offered to buy Jedediah's claim. It so happened they had deeds to nine adjoining claims in Slick Rock, Colorado, the place Budd had said he wanted to go back to. They would do a simple barter—those nine claims for Jedediah's claim.

It took some talking on their part to convince Budd he had a good deal, along with a hundred dollars cash for his moving expenses.

Orville Huggins gazed in awe at Raider. "You sure are the best Pinkerton on the whole national force," he declared. "It just about makes my tummy heave to think I was the one who nearly caused you to quit."

"You *did* cause me to quit, Huggins," Raider snapped in irritation. "Don't start again. Make yourself useful. Send off that stuff to Chicago."

"That's right," Jedediah Budd put in. "And tell them I'm waiting here for the reward."

Orville looked wonderingly at the deeds to the nine claims

in Slick Rock, the forged documents they had been sent to find. "I just can't believe you got them all just as easy as that. What we been looking for all this time." He shook his head. "And you got them just like that. It's real good work, Raider, and I'm sure going to tell them so back in head-quarters."

"Screw headquarters," Raider muttered.

"That ain't no way for a career Pinkerton to talk," Orville reprimanded him. "I'm your friend, but you don't know who might be listening who might report back some of the things you say."

"That's why I say 'em," Raider snarled.

As usual Orville was oblivious to Raider's mood. He kept on pecking away. "What about Buckley and Harewood? Ain't we going to arrest them and take them to court?"

Raider looked at him in distaste. "I didn't come out here to Nevada to make it safe for the likes of you. Way I'd have it, I'd prefer them two walking about free men than the likes of you poking your nose in out west. They built cities back east to hold your sort."

Orville tittered nervously.

"Whyn't you go mail those deeds to Chicago so they can send me my reward," Jedediah put in by way of a peace-maker.

After Orville had gone out the hotel lobby into the street, Raider said, "I swear I could sit back and watch that man die, even if he is a fellow Pinkerton."

Raider spotted an item in that day's North Fork *Gazette* which he pointed out to Jedediah as they sat in the hotel lounge with its big overstuffed leather armchairs, each with a shining brass spitoon next to it.

Budd waved the newspaper away. "I never got around to doing much more than numbers and maybe signing my name."

"I wouldn't have neither," Raider said, "except I had this old battle-ax for a teacher when I was a kid down in Arkansas. With her, it was either learn or die. She damn near killed me before she won out in the end. Listen to this. Its headline says 'Mystery Gold Find.'

Four Chinamen who had held menial positions in our community for some months showed up unexpectedly at the State Assay Office yesterday. An observer has told us that they handed in a large quantity of gold nuggets and were paid for the same in U.S. greenbacks. An inquiry concerning the value of the gold traded to the Assay Office was met with a rebuff by an assay official. The four Chinese were last seen riding out of town westward, laughing and talking among themselves. When asked if he expected his Asian worker to return to the kitchen of his North Fork restaurant, the owner thought it doubtful. When asked if he knew where the Chinamen might have found the gold, he said it certainly was not in his kitchen.

Jedediah Budd turned purple and then deathly white while Raider read this to him.

He gave a kind of strangled laugh. "Come on, you're kidding me, Raider. That's not what it really says!"

Raider handed him the paper. "Go ask someone else what it says."

Budd put the paper down and shook his head sadly. "This won't be the first time in my life that I was robbed, Raider." Suddenly his mood of resignation changed and he began banging his fist on the table and muttering "sons of bitches" over and over again.

Orville Huggins returned and looked at Jedediah in surprise. He said, "Someone told me on the street that Boyle wanted to see me. I'm going up there now."

Raider raised an eyebrow. "After he shot you the last time you went there?"

"That was a mistake," Orville explained earnestly. "I mistook him for Buckley or Harewood, and he mistook me for one of their hired goons. I didn't handle the situation very well—I'm not sure I identified myself clearly. Then I panicked. He shot me in the posterior while I was escaping."

"You going back to give him a better shot at you this time?" Raider asked. "I sure hope he doesn't miss."

Orville sniffed with annoyance, turned on his heel, and went out the lobby door. Raider watched him idly through the window as he clumsily mounted his horse and held onto the saddle pommel for dear life as the horse moved slowly down the street.

Budd was still cursing under his breath. Raider sighed, drained his coffee cup, and got to his feet.

"What about you? Don't you care?" Budd asked him fiercely. "You nearly had all that gold in your own hands, and you lost it!"

Raider smiled and picked up his hat. "If I cared much about gold, Jed, I'd never have become a Pinkerton."

Orville Huggins felt scared, but he reminded himself that he was a Pinkerton operative and flicked the reins against his horse's neck. It was near sundown and the miners were quitting, some dragging their heavy bodies to a meal of sowbelly, beans, and sourdough heated over an open fire, along with strong coffee, and others heading with a light step after the day's heavy work toward the saloons, gaming tables, and whores in North Fork.

Orville's ass still hurt where he had taken the small-caliber derringer bullet. This time crazy Boyle might aim for his head. What was he coming out here for? He didn't have to. Boyle hadn't hired any Pinkertons. Was he going just to show Raider and Jedediah that he had the guts to go back? Orville figured that had to be it, because now that he had time to think about it, he didn't feel it was such a great idea.

He knew that Raider hoped he would get shot so he could be rid of him. Pinkertons always stuck together, no matter what kind of trouble, and here was his partner hoping he'd get shot! They'd warned him in Chicago before he had left to join Raider. They had told him Raider was an animal. They were right.

The sun was low in the sky by the time he reached the deserted diggings owned by Buckley and Harewood. In the middle of them he could see Boyle's claim, with its barricade of scrap lumber around the shaft and cabin which prevented sharpshooters from picking him off as he worked. Boyle rarely left his claim; he brought in fresh supplies only a couple of times during the season, as if he were away someplace in the mountains instead of four or five miles outside the town of North Fork.

A warning shot was fired. Orville heard the bullet whistle through the air high over his head. He saw the flame from the rifle muzzle in the deep shadow of the barricade.

"Boyle!" he roared. "You were the one who sent for me to come here. It's me! Orville Huggins."

"Keep off, Huggins," the barricaded miner bawled. "I didn't send for no Pinkertons—'specially not for one like you."

"I thought you needed my help," Orville shouted lamely while he dismounted.

Boyle gave a loud laugh and showed his head and shoulders. "Only time I'll ask for your help will be to put flowers on my grave. Someone's making a fool of you, boy, sending you out here. If I was you, I'd watch my back. And this time it won't be me shooting at you. Now, get back to town while there's still some light."

"Yes, sir," Orville said obediently.

Huggins hadn't walked more than three paces when two shots rang out and he fell to the ground and lay still.

"Goddamn you, you murdering bastards, I didn't shoot that man," Boyle was yelling from behind his barricade, looking for a shot at whoever it was who had fired on Huggins.

Raider walked calmly over a rise in the ground. "Hold your fire, Boyle," he shouted. "I nailed the whore's scum."

Raider carried his smoking carbine and used his foot to turn over the body of a man with a rifle. "It's Buckley," he announced. "Deader than a doornail. I know you'd like to nail his hide on your barricade, Boyle, but we got to donate his body to the sheriff."

A gust of laughter answered him from behind the barricade. "And who the hell are you?"

Raider told him as he walked toward the motionless body of Orville Huggins, lying face down in the scarred earth of the mine workings.

He poked Huggins in the ribs with his toe. "Get up, Orville. I hit Buckley before he could draw a bead on you. His shot went wild, so you ain't hit with his bullet. If you're dead, you died of fright."

Orville got slowly to his feet. "I'm wounded," he gasped. "I felt warm blood flowing over me."

Raider looked him over. "By the time we ride back to North Fork, it will be too dark for folks to see you pissed in your pants."

"Christ, he's out to kill me, Raider," Jedediah Budd claimed in an alarmed voice at the bar of the Golden Opportunity. "The only man in North Fork I know Dan Harewood is afeared of is you. So I had to tell him that if he tangled with me, he was tangling with you."

Raider poured him a drink from his whiskey bottle and didn't seem too interested.

Jedediah grabbed him by the arm. "Listen to me, you big lunk. He's found out I cheated him on the claims by saying I found gold nuggets there. He's given me until sundown tonight to raise a thousand dollars to buy back my old claim from him, or else. Someone told him I got money stashed in the bank here. But look at it this way—I get six hundred in that reward from the Pinkertons plus the hundred I took off them in the sale. If I have to give him a thousand, I end up losing three hundred on the deal, along with a lot of sorrow and aggravation. I'm not as young as I used to be, Raider. I gotta think of things like security now."

"Why don't you just shoot the varmint?" Raider asked casually.

"Me? Are you crazy? He's faster than me. Way faster."

"Take it from me, Jed, those guys is all talk and bluster. When it comes to throwing lead, they're amateurs."

"Compared with you, they are," Budd said. "Compared with me, Dan Harewood is deadeye and lightning fast. I ain't no slouch with a handgun, and I've had to take care of myself from time to time, but when I know I'm outclassed, I sit still. Or run. But I can't ride out of town. I'm waiting for my reward."

Raider smiled. "So you're siccing me on him like a mean hound dog."

"Damn right. I told him if he's got any guts or self-respect, he'd pay you back for killing his two friends. You know what he said to me. He said Richmond and Buckley didn't mean shit to him and he owns everything now. So far as he's concerned, he said, you done him a favor. Then he told me again he wants that thousand or he's gonna plug me full of holes, no matter whether I'm your friend or not."

"Well, I suppose on account of you waiting for that Pinkerton reward, it's almost like you was on the payroll, like one of us," Raider conceded. "So I suppose I'll have to look out for you till you collect that cash."

"That's the way I see it too," Jedediah averred.

Orville Huggins strolled into the saloon, his face wreathed in smiles, a Western Union telegram in his hand.

"Time to hit the road, Raider," he said in a jovial voice and passed the telegram to his fellow Pinkerton.

Your materials were received in good order, which concludes your current case. Doc Weatherbee sends word he is in dire need in Hugoton, southwestern Kansas. Proceed there immediately.

Wagner

"I don't think this means you," Raider said to Orville.

Huggins snatched the telegram and read it again. "Sure it does. It's addressed to both of us. We go there as partners, Raider. Like we came here."

Raider muttered something under his breath.

Orville Huggins was one thing, but him in combination with Doc Weatherbee would be more than it was fair to ask any man to take. Raider wouldn't deny that Doc was a good operative, as good as or even better in his own way than Raider himself was. It was just that Doc's self-assurance, the way women fell for him all the time, especially women that Raider wanted for himself, the way he did everything according to the Pinkerton rule book—in some ways he was worse than Huggins. But unlike Orville, he was not a dangerous fool. Raider had to grant him that.

Not the two of them together. Raider couldn't take *that*.

What had he done to deserve this treatment from Chicago? Sure, he'd been messy a few times with killings and fires and all, and he hadn't mentioned exactly everything in long-winded reports, but that wasn't any reason to burden a man with not one but two millstones around his neck.

There was one solution. Weatherbee needed his help. Raider was more than willing to give that. The simple answer was that Huggins was not going to Kansas. Raider looked at his fellow Pinkerton's friendly, expectant face and decided that telling him wouldn't do any good. He'd think Raider was only kidding him.

"I was just telling Raider," Jedediah said to Orville, anxious to get back to the subject closest to his heart, "that Harewood is going to kill me unless I give him a thousand dollars by sundown. He says I cheated him on the claim."

"Well, you did," Orville said judgmentally.

"That's what Raider told me to do so I could get the Pinkerton reward! Are you suggesting that I be left to die now that you got your damn papers safely at your head office?"

"No, certainly not," Orville told him sternly. "I'll personally look out for you."

Budd was taken aback. "Orville, that's not what I meant. I can take care of myself better than you could. I don't want you involved—I mean, you might get hurt or something. Or get us both killed. No offense."

Orville looked hurt. "I guess this needs straightforward action," he said and stomped out of the saloon.

"Raider, you can't let him go," Budd said. "Harewood will make salt pork of him."

"Good," Raider grunted. "That way I'll be rid of him."

It turned out Raider guessed right when he figured that Orville Huggins had no intention of calling down Dan Harewood in a gunfight. Instead Orville had complained to the marshal of North Fork and to anyone else who would listen to him—and not many would—that murder was brewing. By this time he was a joke in the town, and some men mockingly recommended that Orville make Dan Harewood "another notch on his gun."

Besides, everyone had a more important thing to think about. It so happened that this was the day when the two local champion jack burros were to be squared off, and thousands of dollars and even mining claims were being wagered on the outcome of the fight.

Dan Harewood was in the crowd, but he too had more important things to take care of than to bother with either Jedediah or Orville, although the latter tried to speak to him several times. Each time Harewood listened for a few moments until he realized that Huggins was not trying to place a bet on the burro fight, and then each time he shook his head impatiently and turned away, shouting the odds he was offering and holding a wad of greenbacks in one hand and a bag of gold coins in the other.

The two animals were goaded first and then released in the desert outside town, penned in only by the crowd of miners, who were talking excitedly while anxiously examining how belligerent was the attitude of their chosen beast. One of the burros was taller and leaner than the other, and he bared the long teeth on his powerful jaws at the other, then charged, reached under his opponent's head, and savagely bit into his neck. The burro kept his teeth clamped into the hide on his opponent's neck as the afflicted animal squealed, bled, and tried to buck free.

Raider was poked in the side by an elbow. It was Budd.

"I bet the thousand I owe Harewood with him, double or quits, on the big animal," Jedediah said happily.

"I picked him too," Raider said. "Since I never win a bet, I think you're out of luck wagering on the same one as me."

"Rip his windpipe out!" Budd yelled to the big burro.

Even if the animal could have understood, he didn't hear because of the roar of triumph from the crowd and the even louder curses and insults at the bleeding animal. Then, in a sudden twist, the smaller animal freed himself, turned his tail toward his oppressor, and caught him with both hind hooves in a mightly blow to the side of the head. The impact of the hooves on the skull bone was as loud and clean as an ax striking wood.

The big animal staggered on his four legs. Then both burros rounded on each other with mouths wide agape, searching for an opening and clashing with their teeth, which made a sound like china breaking.

The large burro was again the fastest, though he seemed to have had much of the fight knocked out of him by the blow to his head. He tore a gouge in the flank of the other animal, which reared on his hind legs and struck back with flailing forelegs.

The vicious duel continued between the two jack burros. They raised a huge plume of dust over the late afternoon desert, and the closer onlookers were coated with the dust raised by the animals' hooves as the fighting burros maneuvered, charged, and dug in to gain traction. At times, overenthusiastic miners got thrown off their feet by the sides or rumps of the heaving animals, which were both too blinded by rage and pain now to be aware of anything but their own combat. The smaller beast's hide was ripped and bleeding from a dozen places. Yet this animal's deadly kicks had obviously concussed his bigger opponent. Without warning, the fight was suddenly over.

The larger burro turned tail and ran. The crowd parted as the animal fled with his smaller combatant in pursuit across the open desert.

The winners cheered; the losers booed. As the crowd began to head back into town toward the saloons, bets were paid off, and huge sums of money changed hands cheerfully.

Jedediah Budd stuck real close to the big, mustached Pinkerton in his battered black Stetson, leather jacket, and faded jeans. It didn't do him any good, because nothing could keep Dan Harewood away from him now.

"The bank's still open," Harewood said to Budd, ignoring Raider, even though he was the man who had killed his two partners. "I'll walk you there, Jed, and we'll settle this debt like gentlemen. I know you got more than enough cash on deposit to cover the two thousand you owe me."

Harewood was talking politely, but there was no mistaking the menace and sinister undertone in his voice. A Colt .45 Peacemaker hung on his right hip.

Budd hid behind Raider.

Raider smiled in his most relaxed way. Anyone who knew him was aware this was a danger signal.

He spoke in an easygoing way. "I think you got one end of a misunderstanding here, mister."

"He bet me double or quits on what he owed me," Harewood growled.

"Jed didn't owe you nothing in the first place," Raider pointed out. "You gave him bum deeds on those claims back in Slick Rock, Colorado. At least some of them are forgeries, and others were altered and what not. Besides, there's a bunch of easterners who claim they agreed to buy the claims. You say Budd owes you money on that. I say he owes you nothing. And double or quits nothing still makes nothing. Now move on, mister, you're in my way."

Out of the corner of his eye, Raider noticed Jedediah slip away. He cursed him silently.

Raider heard the gunshot explode a few feet behind his back, knew the bullet could not have been meant for him, and never let his eyes wander for a moment from those of Dan Harewood.

He saw Harewood's gaze drop for that telltale instant as he went for his gun, hoping Raider had lost his concentration because of the shot behind him.

Raider's gun hand hit the wood handle of his long-barrel Remington and hauled the iron out of its leather holster. The gun jumped quick and easy in his grasp, as if it were light and the movement effortless. Even before the closest bystanders realized what was happening and had a chance to take a step back, the big gleaming barrel of the Remington was leveled in the air, the hammer snapped back, and the trigger pulled.

Dan Harewood's Colt Peacemaker had barely cleared leather when flame spat from the Remington's muzzle and the .44 slug snapped through a rib and stopped him in mid-action. The Colt dangled from his right hand, and his knees buckled. He had hit the dust before the crowd knew what had happened.

Raider swung about, gun at the ready, the hammer pulled back for a new shot, to see what had happened behind him. Jedediah stood with a smoking six-gun over a still figure crumpled in the dust. A handgun lay next to the man's head.

"He tried to backshoot you, Raider," Budd said. "He musta been a backup for Harewood while he was handling bets on the fight."

"Glad you were there," Raider said. "I thought for a moment you had taken off. By the way, where the hell is Orville?"

Budd grinned. "When he saw that the two jack burros were going to be matched, he went back into town. He said he can't stand cruelty to animals."

Next day the Pinkerton money order came in for Budd and he stashed it in the bank.

"Where're you heading now?" Raider asked.

"I was thinking of Virginia City. Maybe even San Francisco."

"Do me a favor, Jed. Take that horse's ass Huggins with you."

Raider wasn't kidding. He persuaded Budd to tell Orville that he, Raider, was traveling separately and under cover while they were to travel together. Orville was in such a tizzy about his baggage that he never noticed the train was going west instead of east. Raider watched it disappear over the horizon with a new, intensifying sense of peace.

He had four hours to wait in Elko before the eastbound train to Salt Lake City was due. After that it would be a long haul by rail down to Kansas. A man had to grab a bit of fun where and when he could. He strode purposefully toward the nearest saloon.

CHAPTER FOUR

The herd managed to reach near Hugoton by late afternoon, and the trail boss rode ahead to find a good place to bed down the cattle for the night. There were 3,300 half-wild Texas steers in the herd, enough to level the town of Hugoton if they stampeded through it.

He found a large hollow in the plain, thick with succulent grass and with several pools to water the animals. He went back and guided the others to the place.

While the cook prepared supper, the men set up camp and divided up night duties among themselves. Before sundown all hands rounded up the cattle into as small an area as they could, and then circled them till they quieted down and settled in for the night. When the animals were calm the cowhands left, except for two, who continued to slowly circle the herd and sing to the beeves from time to time to soothe them.

When the other cowhands got out of earshot of the herd,

they whooped and hollered and swore what they were going
to do when they hit town. It had been one hell of a ride all
the way to Kansas from down in Texas, with heat, dust,
strays, stampedes, thirst—most anything a man could name,
they guessed they'd been through it. And it wasn't over yet.
But the worst part was done. They had made it into the
plains of Kansas. For the steers, that meant plentiful grass
and water. For the men, it meant women, booze, and gaming
tables.

In 1865 Jesse Chisholm, part white and part Cherokee,
drove a wagonload of buffalo skins from Texas through the
Indian Territory to a trading post near the grass huts of the
Indian village of Wichita, Kansas. The wheels of the wagon
bit deep into the prairie soil, and these wheel ruts were used
as a guide by the first of many future travelers along what
came to be known as the Chisholm Trail. The first herd,
2,400 Texas longhorns, was driven along this trail in 1867
through Wichita to the railhead of the Union Pacific Railroad
at Abilene, farther north. However, in 1871 the Santa Fe
Railway laid rails to Newton, not so far north of Wichita
as Abilene. Newton then became "cow capital" for a year,
until Wichita itself became a railhead in 1872.

The threat to Wichita's supremacy as cow capital came
not from the railroad extending farther south but from Joseph
F. Glidden's 1867 invention that hit the market in 1874—
barbed wire. Homesteaders could now fence off the open
range and protect the crops on their plowed land. As the
prairie came under cultivation, cattlemen and their cattle
were forced farther west. Mennonite immigrants from Rus-
sia had brought a new variety of wheat with them, called
Turkey Red, which thrived under Great Plains conditions.

The farmers with their plows and barbed wire hadn't
reached Wichita yet, but everyone knew it was only a matter

of time—in spite of cattlemen killing the farmers or ruining their crops. Worse still, the settlers not only dug up the grass, but they also placed their farms right on whatever water holes were about.

The Chisholm Trail was not like a wagon trail, which was usually only a well-beaten pathway over the smoothest and least challenging terrain. There was no single trail. The first herds grazed over the land as they traveled, so later herds had to be driven to either side, where grass was still available. The more cattle driven, the wider, dustier, and barer the wide strip became, until huge areas of land were consumed.

"Them goddamn nesters is going to string their wire all over," Tom Murdock complained in the First and Last saloon in Hugoton, down in the southwest corner of Kansas, near the borders of Colorado and the Indian Territory. The place was called the First and Last because it was the first place cowhands could buy a drink on the drive north after the long dry stretch, and it was the last place to get a drink on the way back to Texas.

"Them shithead nesters will make it all the way out to here in time," Murdock went on grumbling over his drink. "'Cept you and I will be long gone afore they plow the grass under around here. Even though I'll be six foot under in the dirt, it's still going to bother my bones to have farmers walking around on top instead of real men like us ranchers, cowboys, drovers, and buffalo hunters. Hell, I'd sooner give this land back to the Injuns than have them homesteaders cutting it up."

Murdock was a tall lean man with leathery skin and not an ounce of fat. His long bony fingers gripped his whiskey glass, and he threw the burning fluid down his throat. His two companions sharing the bottle at the bar were as weather-beaten as he. One was as lean and bony as Murdock but

pint-sized—his name was Rob Lynch. The third man was
Jim Coulter, who was of average size, with big hands, a
barrel chest, and a red fleshy face.

The First and Last saloon didn't do a fancy trade. It had
its share of city-schooled gamblers and ladies of easy virtue,
but even they knew this was no place to put on airs—
misunderstandings and sudden dislikes could be dangerous
at the First and Last. Most of the customers were cowboys,
with a few buffalo hunters standing out among them because
they liked to wear buckskin jackets and breeches like old-
time plainsmen and scouts. Wild Bill Hickok had given up
his fringed and beaded buckskins and stalked about, as
marshal of Abilene, in a Prince Albert coat, an embroidered
vest, and checked pants, with a silk-lined cape and a pair
of silver-mounted pearl-handled revolvers. With a hundred
killings to his name, no one was going to comment on Wild
Bill's sense of fashion.

Hugoton had no strong marshal like Wild Bill in Abilene.
Men came and went, and if some stranger got shot for
something, it was no big deal. The friends of the man who
did the shooting would say it was in self-defense—and if
there were those who wanted to differ, that could lead to
another fight. Marshals came and went too. There were
easier places than Hugoton for a lawmaker to make a living.

"Seems like a mighty big herd coming this way, just
judging from the dust they're raising," Rob Lynch opined.
He did not let the small size of his body interfere with the
great volume he drank.

"You suggesting we go in together to make an offer?"
Tom Murdock asked.

"That's why we're sitting here together, ain't it?" Lynch
replied.

All three men earned a good living from buying Texas
longhorn herds from the drovers, holding them a while to

fatten on the rich Kansas grass, and then turning a nice profit when they themselves drove the cattle to the railhead or in turn sold them to other middlemen. Lately they had been buying jointly. Any one of them could easily have afforded to buy any size herd on his own—this was not the reason they banded together. First, they didn't have to bid against one another, as the three biggest buyers in Hugoton, when they bought jointly. And second, the herd would not be stampeded and stolen so easy during the time it was out on grass if all three of them put their men guarding it and none of the three had anything to gain from the misfortune of the others.

They would never go so far as to accuse each other of cattle thieving, but each of them believed with good reason that the others had stolen from him in times past. Nowadays, bygones were bygones. It was more important for them to see eye to eye with one another in order to rake the dollars in. Feuding with each other only cost them money.

"Who's the fella down the bar with the gray derby?" Murdock asked.

"A quack," Jim Coulter said. "He drove into town this morning with a wagonload of medicines. Calls hisself Doc Weatherbee. He's staying over at the Eagle Hotel."

"I don't like the looks of him," Murdock observed. "He seems more like a gambler or something than a doctor."

Coulter shrugged. "So don't play cards with him."

The man they were talking about sure stood out from the rough and ready crowd in the saloon. Apart from his carefully brushed pearl gray derby with a curled brim, he wore a checkered worsted wool suit, a silk shirt, a peacock blue vest, and five-button Melton overgaiters. The cowhands in their chaps, sweat-stained shirts, and spurred boots poked fun at this stranger from time to time, and he seemed to take it in the best of spirits, caring little for anyone's opinion of him. There was one thing about this Doc Weatherbee that gained other men's respect and envy—women fluttered about him like moths around a lighted lamp on a dark night.

Nothing much happened in Hugoton that Tom Murdock, Rob Lynch, and Jim Coulter didn't know about. They made it their business to know—and control—everything. This itinerant physician was only a minor detail that caught Tom Murdock's eye as not quite fitting into the usual pattern of things.

"Now that we're working together," Murdock told the others, "so long as we don't backstab each other, we can get to trust each other and join together to put Hugoton on the map. Like Joe McCoy was the one to make Abilene a cowtown. Once the railhead reached there, he saw the possibilities. He built the stockyards on the eastern edge of town, big enough to hold three thousand beeves. Then he advertised in Texas newspapers, and soon enough the big herds started coming up the Chisholm Trail. All right, Newton and then Wichita stole Abilene's thunder. But who's going to steal Wichita's thunder? Sure as hell, the nesters is going to wire off the place, and who's going to get the cattle trade? Are we going to let Dodge City take everything just because they got the Santa Fe tracks in their town? I say no. We're south of Wichita, Dodge City, and all the others. The cattle pass through Hugoton to get to any of those goddamn places. I say we three bring the railroad here and make Hugoton cow capital of the world!"

Lynch and Coulter looked a bit bored. They had heard all this a thousand times before. They were well into their plans to make Hugoton the northern terminus of the Chisholm Trail, and they saw no reason why they had to listen to Murdock, every time he had a couple of drinks, act as if the idea had just occurred to him. It hadn't been Murdock's idea in the first place—Lynch had thought of it and brought

the three of them together. Murdock was beginning to be-
have as if he was the senior of the three partners, and Lynch
and Coulter didn't like it.

They looked carefully when they heard a dispute down
along the bar. This saloon was the kind of place where a
wise man followed the progress of arguments so he knew
when to duck if lead started flying. Drunken cowhands killed
almost as many by accident as they did on purpose. The
cowhands didn't wield their weapons expertly like professional gunmen, and yet they were often more willing to
settle a row with a shooting iron than a skilled gunslinger.

This dispute involved the elegantly dressed quack they
had noticed before and a staggering drunk drover who was
looking for a fight. The three cattlemen watched as the
drover shouted insults and made mock fast draws against
the unarmed Doc Weatherbee. And they saw how in the
middle of this Weatherbee managed, by sleight of hand, to
pull the drover's Colt six-gun from its holster and slip it to
one of the drover's friends, thus making them part of the
joke too.

Then they all swallowed their drinks and enjoyed the
sight of the drover make a fool of himself by posturing as
a badman until he discovered his empty holster. He blamed
his friends, not Doc Weatherbee, for this and wanted to fight
all of them. One of them persuaded him to leave along with
them to try another saloon, knowing the drover would forget
everything as soon as he was out the door. They bought
Doc a drink before they left.

"You see the way this quack Weatherbee handled that?"
Murdock asked the others. "Mark my words, keep an eye
on him so long as he stays in this town."

Nine cowhands, trail dust stuck to their skin and clothes
with sweat, burst through the batwing doors of the First and

Last saloon. Those nearest the bar laughed good-humoredly and made way for them. Most men in the place knew what the feeling was like to finally hit a saloon after weeks on the trail. The gamblers and whores paid them little mind as yet, knowing that these men had not been paid off. Whatever cash they had would go on drinks. But if Murdock or any of the others made a deal with their trail boss, the men would be paid off in Hugoton and stay on some days to live it up and blow their pay before heading back to Texas. Then the gamblers and whores would have their hands full.

The new arrivals threw back the cheap scorching whiskey, refilled their glasses, and threw back some more. They grew talkative.

"Few nights back we bedded down the herd at the lower end of a valley stream in the Indian Territory. There was a couple of herds up-valley from us, resting up. In the middle of the night, in pitch darkness, we hear this great thundering sound. And it's coming our way! I was one of the night-hawks guarding our herd, and I see our beeves start wanting to run. Them animals was no fools. They didn't want to just stand there and get stomped on by those other herds charging up the valley. So they took off. We spent all next day, from sunup to sundown, separating them damn herds from one another till we had our drove together again. But now the beeves are in the mood for running, so that night our drove takes off again. This time they don't meet no others. What happens is we lose three men and four hundred cows. Gone. Vanished. So after we been in the saddle all night, we keep the drove in place for the day and hunt down those men and steers. We find them near twenty miles away, half dead of thirst and lost. We don't reach the herd till after dawn the next day, and then we pull out and travel all day. By this time we ain't counting time in the saddle by hours— I don't even know how many *days* I been on them salty mustangs. All I know is I got eight horses in the remuda, and by the time them cows was back together, all eight of them cayuses were sorry-looking critters, broke down and good for nothing. I don't reckon I got more'n two, three hours straight sleep each night for nigh on a week now, and here I go lowering down this rotgut first break I get. It ain't sensible nor reasonable what a man does to himself."

Of course there were others at the bar who felt they could top these stories with trials and tribulations of their own, which got the newcomers to further elaborate on what they had so recently been through and go into other disasters they had forgotten to mention before.

Murdock, Lynch, and Coulter sympathized and waited. It might sound from their stories that the trail boss would be more than anxious to get rid of this troublesome herd quick as he could and at any reasonable price. But the three cattle dealers knew that as soon as they showed interest as buyers, the trail boss would develop a sudden affection for these lean and panicky longhorns, and only a top-dollar price, in his estimation, could separate him from these fat and docile beasts.

Doc Weatherbee was sizing up the town, aware that he in turn was being sized up by some of the denizens of the First and Last saloon. As usual Doc was looking for one particular person and trying to hide the fact that he was— as well as hiding the fact that he was a Pinkerton operative.

Being a Pinkerton was not the healthiest occupation in places like Kansas cowtowns. A man might hold no personal grudge against Doc himself but kill him all the same in order to get back at the Pinkerton National Detective Agency. Allan Pinkerton had been responsible for many outlaws ending their days by dancing on the end of a rope or rotting behind bars with sentences stretching into the next century, should they live that long in prison squalor. Many of these men had sons or comrades who felt it their duty to avenge them somehow, even when they didn't deny that justice had been done. One way to get back at Allan Pinkerton was to destroy one of his personally picked, highly trained operatives—the way he had destroyed their relative or comrade.

So Doc Weatherbee was a traveling physician. He hawked medicines and talked to everyone about their ailments, free to move where he pleased and to watch and act when the time came. And if an itinerant quack hit the saloons to ease the pain of his existence better than any of his harmless, worthless medicines could, he was staying well within the role he had chosen to play.

The immaculately groomed easterner with the Harvard accent was not taken seriously by the roughs at the bar. However, he did arouse the interest and attentions of the "soiled doves" present. One in particular gave him the eye, a woman in her late twenties whose outstanding beauty gave her an imperious air. She sat alone at a table, with a bottle of champagne in a silver ice bucket and a cut crystal goblet before her. Her table was the only one in the place covered by a cloth.

Doc ordered another bottle of champagne for her from where he stood at the bar. She refused it, having glanced haughtily at Doc after the waiter had pointed him out as her would-be benefactor. The men around Doc at the bar snickered at her obvious putdown of him—none of them had the nerve to approach her themselves for fear of being made to look a fool in front of the others. Then the waiter crossed over to Doc and told him that while the lady refused his kind offer of another bottle of champagne, she would be pleased if he would join her to share the one already on her table. The sneers on the faces around Doc dissolved into looks of envy.

She had long straight black hair, dark brown eyes, and a nose way too small for her face and especially for the snooty look she tried to cast on the world. Clad in the latest silk fashions from Paris, which revealed the tops of her pointed breasts and left her shoulders bare, she in her own way was as out of place as Doc Weatherbee in these surroundings. Her fashions would have fitted in an elegant expensive gambling palace in one of the big cowtowns, but here in Hugoton—little more than a short stopoff on the great Chisholm Trail—she was like some exotic tropical bird that has lost its way and flown into more drab surroundings.

"I'm Charlene."

"Doc Weatherbee. Everyone calls me Doc."

Her sinuses bothered her. Doc had just the thing in his medical bag for that, guaranteed to relieve her discomfort. Unfortunately he had left the bag in his room at the Eagle Hotel. He would fetch it for her later.

"There's no hurry. I think it must be the bubbles in the champagne that help keep my sinuses clear right now."

While Doc allowed that this could be true, he had to admit he had not heard of it as a cure before.

They both laughed, and this time she accepted when he suggested another bottle.

Doc had learned the names of some of the prominent local inhabitants, and he carefully spaced his inquiries about them before he slipped in the name Myles Lyman.

"Sure I know Myles," she said with a smile. "Any time he's been to my place, I carefully check to see nothing's missing. He's a charming man—he just can't help trying to get the better of other folk. I think doing bad things to them makes him feel he's better. But he ain't got the better of me yet!"

Doc smiled. "I've heard a lot about him, but I don't think

I've ever set eyes on him. What's he look like?"

She looked about the saloon. "He ain't here right now. He might be later."

Doc let it go at that and quickly changed the subject. "Another one they mention a lot is the tall thin man over there, name of Tom Murdock."

"Oh, I know Mr. Murdock real well too," Charlene said.

Doc noted she didn't call him by his first name as she had done with everyone else so far.

"They say he was just a small-time cattle jobber until a few years ago, and now I hear he could buy out this whole town, lock, stock, and barrel, and have enough money left over to fill a barn. He must have it," she added with a sardonic smile, "'cause he sure don't throw it around in here. He's a man who demands his money's worth and then is slow to pay."

"And he still gets what he wants?"

"Sure thing. Any girl that don't give it to him has got to leave town. Mr. Murdock is a real charming man."

"And those two he's in cahoots with? Lynch and Coulter?"

"What about them? Lynch keeps to himself and stays home with his wife and kids, so far as I know. Coulter's an animal. Likes to beat a girl, I've been warned. I've never been with him, though he's been pressing me hard. Say, what you want to know all this stuff for? I been giving you the rundown on a lotta people in this town. You want to know about the parson next? And then the judge? You one of these newspaper fellas? 'Cause if you are, I can tell you, you say any of the things I told you and these men will come after you and shoot you dead. Serve you right too, I say."

"I'm just interested in folk," Doc said. "A people watcher, that's what you could call me."

"You know, that's not a bad way to be," Charlene said. "Think of all the trouble I'd have stayed out of if I'd just looked instead of touched."

"You'd have been bored."

"True." She laughed. "Talk of the devil, or at least one of them, look who comes here."

Jim Coulter swaggered across the saloon to their table. "Just made ourselves a big deal, Charlene. You see the size of the dust cloud that herd raised outside town earlier today? Well, if all is like the trail boss says it is when we go look see tomorrow morning, all them beeves is going to belong to us."

"Good for you," Charlene said without enthusiasm.

"It could be good for you too, girl, if you treat me right."

"Sorry, Jim, I'm busy."

Coulter gave Doc Weatherbee a sour look. Up till this point he had pretended he wasn't there. Doc gave him a bright smile and Coulter looked away.

"You going to waste your time on trash?" he asked Charlene.

"I wouldn't dream of it," she said, implying that Coulter and not Doc was the trash.

This subtlety was lost on Jim Coulter. "Then git along, girl, and we'll go places."

"Jim, I told you I'm busy."

Coulter threw Weatherbee a mean look. "How long you going to be in town, fella?"

Doc shrugged. "I hadn't thought about it."

"Start thinking about it right now." Coulter stomped back to his friends at the bar.

"I'd watch out for him," Charlene warned Doc. "I didn't mean to get you in any trouble, because he's dangerous."

"I don't easily get in trouble," Doc said calmly.

In a while they left together. When they reached his hotel

room, she had forgotten all about her sinus medicine and seemed more interested in other things.

Doc took her in his arms and kissed her. Then he put her sitting on a table and freed her breasts from the confinement of her low-cut dress. He took a nipple in his mouth, rolled it between his tongue and the roof of his mouth, and sucked on the warm pebble of flesh. She murmured with pleasure and flinched once when he used too much pressure.

As his mouth caressed her breasts, his hands stroked her bare legs under her silk dress. His right hand glided up between her thighs, sliding over her smooth skin. She parted her legs so he could reach her warm welcoming muff. His hand stroked her, and then his fingertips found her moist slit. His finger feathered her clit, and she trembled and writhed under his soft and expert ministrations. She clutched his arm with both hands and dug her fingernails into his skin as she shuddered in a crying, uncontrolled climax.

CHAPTER FIVE

Three men rode out of Hugoton a little before first light. They headed north toward where low rolling swells in the ground, too small to be called hills, were becoming visible on the horizon in the gray light of early morning. They were anxious to leave Hugoton seen by as few as possible, and they relaxed once they were beyond the outskirts of the town. A few freighters had been tending to their teams of six at the livery stables, and a few more were already outside the stores on the main street, loading provisions on their wagons for outlying ranches. The three riders stifled the workingmen's greetings with cold looks that made the freighters and storekeepers turn away as if they had been mistaken in thinking they had seen someone in the first place. They were decent men with families to support and jobs or small businesses to keep. They didn't want to mess with no one. Specially not with Mad Mike, Seattle Bill, and the Kid.

It was the general opinion that Hugoton was no longer a decent or safe place to live since these three had come to town. No one could say much, since the three had been hired by the town council "to maintain law and order." So the council had said, the council of course being Murdock, Lynch, and Coulter. The others who sat on it had been terrorized into voting along with the powerful cattlemen, except for a couple of oddballs whose opposition just went to make things look honest.

Mad Mike balanced his double-barrel shotgun across his saddle and took the lead. He was a washed-out old gunfighter, crazy as a bedbug—and it was this jittery watchfulness that had kept him alive so long. Seattle Bill followed. He was fat and sullen—he didn't say much, he just did things. The Kid tailed along behind, making it plain he wasn't following in anyone's lead but just going along for the convenience of it. He was the one the townspeople of Hugoton feared most. First day in town he'd killed a barkeep for telling him he was too young to drink. Next had been a cowhand who had jeered him about not being old enough to shave. Then another cowhand, no one knew why. Maybe he just felt like it.

The sun had inched up over the sea of green Kansas grass as the three riders neared the spine of low rises.

"Has to be back somewheres this way," Mad Mike called out, pointing east along the hills.

They climbed into the hills until they could see the town of Coronado on the far side, and then they headed east.

"See that big gap down along? I'm betting that's where they hope to lay rails through."

The Kid was grouchy. "Who gives a shit if these little prairie dog towns has railroads or not?"

"The people who pays us gives a shit, and that's enough

for me," Mike philosophized. "Them loons who hired us think they're gonna turn Hugoton into another Wichita. Can you beat that?"

The Kid's harsh laugh showed how much of a joke he thought this was.

Mike went on. "So we just run these railroaders off like they was sheep and tell 'em not to come back. This here is a survey team. They can't lay rails through these hills without these survey boys laying things out in advance for them. We chase these fellas away, word'll get back to the Irishmen putting down the trestles and rails that there's better work for 'em with the Santa Fe to Hugoton. We've got to stop the Missouri Pacific from trying to reach Coronado before the Santa Fe reaches Hugoton."

"I been out that backcountry and there ain't tracks within hundreds of miles of here," the Kid objected. "What're we doing stopping them here?"

"Like I just told you, Kid," Mad Mike said patiently, "the survey boys go ahead of the others for hills and such. They're the ones you have to let know there's trouble ahead for them. Nothing stops the rail setters. They just throw down the trestles and four men pick a rail off a mule-drawn wagon while another four is doing the same thing with their rail's partner. Then along comes a few with sledgehammers and spikers—and in a few minutes flat, that railroad is fifteen feet farther on than before. Hell, I seen them back east in Iowa just throw rails on the hard flat ground so the railroad could get to the next town first and win the government grant. They'll cross that flat prairie to Coronado in hardly no time at all if they don't meet no opposition. And us three is that opposition."

"We make it like they won't want to come out here?" the Kid asked.

"I ain't saying that," Mad Mike went on. "Way I understand it is the Santa Fe and Missouri Pacific is racing each other here for government money and the railhead stockyard business. Right now the Santa Fe is racing to Hugoton, and the Missouri Pacific to Coronado. Our bosses in Hugoton want the Missouri Pacific to be racing to their town, not Coronado. That way no matter which railroad gets there first, Hugoton is the winner. Got it?"

"I still say it don't matter a shit," the Kid responded querulously.

They rode on for more than two hours before they came across the survey team—seven men all told. Two looked through instruments on tripods and directed others where to place wooden stakes.

Seattle Bill pointed. He had spotted two tents in the shade of some trees in the low hills.

Mad Mike nodded to him. "They must have horses back there too."

After Seattle Bill trotted off on his horse toward the camp, Mike and the Kid circled the survey team till they were behind them. Although all three riders were in plain view, the surveyors, immersed in their work, had not yet spotted them. Mike dismounted and began to loosen and uproot the survey stakes the team had already set in the ground. The Kid followed suit.

"Hey!"

They didn't look up when they heard the shout.

"You two! What are you doing there?" Three of the surveyors began walking rapidly toward them.

The Kid stopped his work, ambled to his horse, and pulled a Winchester rifle from the saddle sheath. When the three surveyors saw this, they slowed and then stopped. Their faces turned as they talked with one another. They seemed unsure what to do and remained where they were.

The flames of the tent Seattle Bill set afire caught their attention. One of the three surveyors nearest the Kid started to run toward the camp, shouting and waving his arms at Bill, who was setting fire to the second tent by burning dry grass along one side of it. The Kid dropped the surveyor with a single shot. The man lay still in the grass.

One of the surveyors farthest away from the Kid shot at him with a rifle. The Kid took his time in responding, sighting along the barrel while the surveyor's bullets zipped around him. Again, he had to fire only once—a beautiful shot which caught the surveyor in the center of his chest and laid him low in the grass.

The two surveyors nearest the Kid walked real slow toward their fallen comrade, glancing at the Kid all the time to make sure what they were doing was not annoying him. They stopped for a moment to examine the fallen man, then covered his face with his hat. They walked slowly back to where they had been before.

"I don't know what you got into shooting for," Mad Mike complained. "You shoot one, you gotta shoot them all."

"Naw," the Kid said. "They ain't close enough to know our faces."

"Let's go help Bill chase off their horses."

Up at the camp, Bill was throwing the surveyors' belongings and spare stakes onto the burning tents. Wood was scarce on the prairies—the surveyors had had to carry in these stakes with them for hundreds of miles.

"Quiet, gentlemen, please," the schoolteacher said in a prissy voice. "The council is in session."

The Hugoton town council sat in the schoolhouse, and this the teacher regarded as giving him a certain amount of authority. The mayor, a churchgoing storekeeper and a man of few words, sat at the head of the table. Since the kids had eaten at the table earlier in the day, the councilors had to watch out for sticky substances left either accidentally or purposely adhering to the benches or the table itself. Murdock, Lynch, and Coulter sat along one side of the table. Four men faced them on the other side, and the teacher sat at the lower end, facing the mayor.

Tom Murdock waited impatiently for the mayor to mumble the conventional opening questions to the council's secretary—the teacher—and for the minutes of the last meeting to be adopted unread.

"Now listen here." Murdock waved a bony finger at the table in general. "I got me something important to say. This town issued bonds to put up money for improvements so Hugoton can become the county seat. Once we get to be the county seat, we can control everything that comes into this county—including anything that's on its way to Coronado. Like a railroad, for instance. Don't put that in the minutes of this meeting, you dumb bastard, or the state people will have us up on conspiracy charges. Now what I want to say is this. These here bonds were selling real well in Topeka and other places back east until a few weeks ago. Then they got competition and no one bought much anymore. Sure Coronado has a bond issue as well as us, but we're favorites to become the county seat, so I knew the competition wasn't coming from their bonds. Then I learned who it was. Right here in Hugoton, sitting right here among us, we got this snake in the grass selling lots in a new town he's organizing."

This was greeted by a stunned silence. The Hugoton town council was familiar with the treachery and competition of Coronado, the only other town within a handy distance. The prospect of another town springing up could only be seen as a threat to Hugoton's future supremacy—and to their own well-being.

A chorus of voices shouted questions at Tom Murdock, who basked in this glow of attention and took his own sweet time in satisfying their curiosity.

"The sale of lots for this new town has affected our bond issue—and that's supposing there was room for a new town hereabouts, which there ain't." Murdock went on some more about the problems they were facing, then he named names. "You see that citified dude from back east who has been hanging about town? The one in the gray suits and the silver-tipped cane, who has the buckboard with the striped sun-shade. Lyman is his name. Myles Lyman. He's one of these land speculators, and he's hoping to start this new town and fill it with farmers from back east and all kinds of foreign immigrant riffraff. They'll be stretching barbwire across the grassland hereabouts even before they get to Wichita if we let this Myles Lyman have his way. But that ain't all. Even if there was room for this new town—and I already said there ain't—he's messing up our bond issue by underselling us and making his new town look like a better buy than Hugoton."

"Where the hell is this new town?" one councilor asked in a puzzled voice.

"It doesn't exist except on paper," Murdock cackled, admiring the concept in spite of himself. "Them dang fool Easterners don't know no better. Once they got their piece of paper, they're happy."

By this time Doc Weatherbee had checked into things and found he was wasting his time. There were no laws in the state of Kansas against what Myles Lyman was doing, nor was he breaking any federal regulations. There was no way for Doc to put a hand on him.

Doc had sent a telegram to Chicago headquarters about this and had expected to be reassigned. Instead he got the following immediate response:

Clients in Cleveland expect you to persist.

Wagner

This was not what Doc wanted at all. He was not an impatient man, the sort who quit if he didn't get fast results in an investigation. He just didn't see much possibilities in this case. Myles Lyman was one of those smooth operators who stayed just inside written law while violating all codes of ethics, honesty, and decency. The federal and various state governments were too interested in expanding westward to bother with the various sharp practices that had sprung up with the new land boom west of the Mississippi.

Besides, the clients in Cleveland who expected him to persist, according to Wagner's telegram, were motivated by only one thing—revenge. They wanted to see Lyman behind bars or, better still, dead because he had cheated them.

This scheme had involved land in the state of Kansas. Myles Lyman purchased a square mile of land, divided it into town lots, and recorded the plot at the county seat under the name of Ohio City. Then he went back east to Cleveland, Ohio, with maps of the town on which nonexistent buildings were marked. He said what the new town needed more than money was a supply of hardworking settlers, and to persuade them to come out to Kansas and settle in Ohio City, he would give town lots away free to ambitious and willing men. All they had to do was pay a notary ten dollars for recording the deed and the town lot was theirs to build on or use as they saw fit. Big numbers jumped at this opportunity. Lyman's profit, of course, was in the notary fees he collected for 2,500 "choice town lots." Nothing was ever built on the site. Later the Kansas county sold the land for unpaid taxes, and thus Ohio City was born and died without ever having lived.

Doc had heard that a few disgruntled investors who had made the trip from Cleveland out to Kansas were embittered enough by the experience to make a collection back in Cleveland and deliver the money collected to Allan Pinkerton with the sole instruction to keep after Myles Lyman while the money lasted or until something could be pinned on him. Apparently what Doc had heard was true. He was going to be left out here until he found something to hang around Lyman's neck.

It didn't even occur to Doc to try to set up Lyman with false evidence. Doc Weatherbee did everything by the book and scrupulously observed every Pinkerton regulation, of which there were many. He would stay here in Kansas as instructed until Myles Lyman made a slip. Then Weatherbee would get him.

But Lyman was wary. He had been operating for a long time and knew all the ins and outs of real estate scams. The earliest fraud Doc had detected Lyman's hand in had been way back in 1857. It had particularly caught Doc's attention because R. J. Gatling was also involved. Gatling went on later to invent the Gatling gun, of which Doc had two concealed in a secret compartment at the bottom of his wagon. The Gatling gun's multiple revolving barrels allowed an unbelievably rapid rate of fire without any single barrel becoming dangerously overheated. It had been an unpleasant surprise to Doc to find Gatling's name linked to that of Myles Lyman, yet there it was.

A group of promoters, Lyman and Gatling among them, chose the site for the town of White Cloud on Indian land with the expectation that the Indians would soon be moved from Kansas. They encouraged others to build on town lots, although the Indians could technically have seized the buildings and sold them before being forced to leave. They didn't. When the land was officially opened for settlement, the group of promoters bought everything from the government and announced a big auction for July 4. The owners of buildings in the town were told they would have to acquire the deeds to their lots at this auction.

Lyman, Gatling, and their friends laid on a barbecue, booze, music, and patriotic speeches. They hired actors, circus people, and drifters to pretend to be interested investors and to bid at the auction. Special paddleboats came upstream and downstream on the Missouri for the big holiday sale. They sold 6,000 boat tickets and made more than $20,000 on travel, entertainment, food, and drink. They made an equal sum on land sales to the visitors. The lots with valuable buildings already standing on them they bought for themselves by bidding ridiculously high prices for land they already owned—thus depriving the building's constructor of his property. They ended up with all the most valuable lots in White Cloud, as well as a hefty cash profit.

Doc sat at a table in the First and Last saloon and glanced across to where Myles Lyman sat, nursing a drink and reading a newspaper. Lyman was about sixty. He dressed in the style of a riverboat gambler, but his gray hair and elderly ways made him seem more grandfatherly than the predator he was in reality. Yet his eyes were sharp, and his glance lively. Also, he was jealous as hell because Doc had stolen Charlene.

Myles Lyman wasn't the only man in town who resented the way Doc Weatherbee monopolized Charlene's time. Doc knew he was not too popular in Hugoton because of this— no place took kindly to a stranger who walked in and took over the prettiest girl in town. But it amused Doc to bother

Myles Lyman in this way. Especially since Doc could pin nothing else on him.

Lyman's present scheme involved a town called Smallwood in Comanche County. The town had voted a $72,000 bond issue, and these bonds were now on sale in Topeka and points east. When Doc visited the place, he found that Comanche County was open prairie with grazing cattle herds and that Smallwood consisted of two timber shacks, without doors or windows. One shack was used occasionally by a buffalo hunter. Apparently this man and Myles Lyman were the total population of the "town," and it was they who had voted the bond issue.

The Kansas attorney general, A. L. Williams, wanted to prosecute, but other powers in the state felt that such a trial could give all Kansas town bond issues a bad name—so they said. Nothing was done. Nothing would be done. It was now up to the Pinkertons to trap Lyman and to insist on his prosecution. Doc kept his identity as a Pinkerton operative secret and tried to conceal his special interest in the real estate trickster. All Weatherbee could do was remain observant and pounce when, and if, an opportunity was offered. In the meantime he decided he might as well enjoy himself while he waited.

When Charlene entered the saloon, Doc waved to her from his table. As she walked in, Myles Lyman stood and suggested that she join him—only to be ignored as if he weren't there. Jim Coulter scowled in Doc's direction from where he stood at the bar.

When Charlene and Doc Weatherbee left the First and Last, they went to her house, which was a two-room log cabin near the edge of town. She had covered the wood beams of the inside walls with stretched cloth, had hung drapes, put down carpets and rugs, and lit the place up by cut glass lamps with silver mountings, so it looked like a luxury suite on Nob Hill instead of a cabin on the edge of a prairie cowtown.

Doc took one round, firm globe of her breasts in his right hand.

"Don't waste much time, do you?" she asked and pushed him away in order to take off her hat. She playfully threatened him with a long, deadly hat pin when he approached her from behind.

In a few quick and expert moves, she slipped out of her silk gown and stood naked before the full-length mirror, critically examining her body.

"I don't know what you see in me, Doc," she said, fishing for compliments. "It often puzzles me."

"It's your face, my dear. Your sincere expression and the color of your eyes." Doc could no longer keep his gaze averted from her body, even if he knew it was making her frantic for his attention. He touched her nipples with his fingertips, then ran his hands down the front of her body until the curls of her bush were caught between his fingers.

Then he sought the long, smooth stretch of her thigh, stroking the creamy skin of her legs and wandering back up over her belly.

Her hand felt the bulge in his pants and tugged urgently at his belt buckle.

Doc shucked his clothes in a hurry—well, in what could be called a hurry for him. He didn't throw them anyplace on the floor like any other man would, but he didn't pause either to check on the creases as he normally would.

The wait had made Charlene hotter. When at last he lay on her bed beside her, she almost whimpered. "Come inside me quick, Doc, I can't stand it no more!"

Doc, ever the gentleman, was pleased to oblige. He guided

the head of his swollen organ into the opening of her sex and slid inside her, deeper and deeper, feeling the rippling pressure on his cock.

She groaned, spread her legs wider, and heaved against him rhythmically. His throbbing member relentlessly thrust into her innermost being, as she dissolved in passion beyond her control beneath his masterful play.

Myles Lyman left the First and Last saloon in disgust not long after Charlene and Doc. This had not been a good day. Apart from being put down again by Charlene in favor of that snake oil salesman she had taken a fancy to—Myles was damn sure the so-called Doc Weatherbee would have no genuine college degree, if he took the trouble to check, which he wouldn't bother to do because he had more important things to attend to—apart from being ignored by Charlene again, he had received bad news at the Western Union office. One of his commissioned dealers in Smallwood town bonds had been shot dead while making a sale the previous evening in Topeka.

He could have passed off the shooting as an unfortunate happening unrelated to his enterprise had not a second bond salesman been attacked that very morning, also in Topeka. This was the man who had sent him the telegram, which, besides giving the news of the other man's death, described the close brush with death the second man had had and the shouted warning to him that he mightn't be so lucky the next time if he tried to sell Smallwood bonds again. The telegram closed with the man's resignation. Myles couldn't blame him.

One other thing in the telegram bothered Lyman. "Watch out for yourself. They will be looking for you," the message read. It was not a threat but a warning. Why would they be looking for him? He wasn't actively selling Smallwood bonds himself. He had left that to others, feeling that the sales commission he had to pay his salesmen was well worth it to keep himself at a little distance from the operation in case things went sour all of a sudden.

He hadn't gone much more than twenty yards into the darkness out of the lighted area in front of the saloon, when a fist cracked against the side of his head and he fell dazed on the dusty ground. He took a glancing blow from a boot in his rib cage and was dragged face down by the collar of his coat into a pitch black alley between two closed and shuttered stores.

"Shoot the bastard!"

"Hold off awhile, Kid," a more mature voice continued. "He's got some things to tell us."

Myles was toed in the side.

"Gittup!"

Myles recognized the Kid's voice as he picked himself off the ground. The other voice belonged to Mad Mike. Somewhere, silent in the darkness, the surly one they called Seattle Bill would be standing, quiet but equally willing to pull a trigger as the skittery crazy one they called the Kid. Myles wondered what they wanted with him. He'd been careful always to steer clear of them, to give them no cause for any bad feeling toward him. Myles had seen these boys in action, and he didn't like what he saw at all.

Then Myles remembered the telegram. *Watch out for yourself. They will be looking for you.* So that was it! All the stuff about the salesman's lucky escape had been bullshit. The salesman had bought his life by informing on Myles. Then he had had an attack of the guilts and telegraphed that warning, without admitting openly what he had done. Damn! It was all there, between the lines. Myles felt he must be getting careless. Or old. He shouldn't have missed it. Now it was his turn. They had come for him.

"Lyman, you low skunk, you better listen careful, 'cause I'm going to say this just once." It was Mad Mike's voice, level and menacing. "You been messing with raising funds for some other town while you sit here in Hugoton pretending to be one of us. Can you give me one reason—just one—why the Kid shouldn't put a slug in your brain?"

Myles didn't need time to think. "Because it ain't me who's putting out them bonds for Smallwood, over in Comanche County. That's what you're talking about, ain't it?"

"That's the place," Mad Mike agreed.

"It ain't me. I just work for him. I'm a hired hand. Just like you boys. I got to do all the shit work and take the rap for whatever goes wrong, pretend it's me who owns everything so I can protect the real boss. He just sits back and laughs at you all and rakes in the money."

The Kid burst out, "I'm gonna kill this fast-talking sidewinder—"

"Easy there, Kid," Mad Mike cautioned. "You feel like telling us who this boss of yours is, Lyman?"

"You know him," Myles said.

"What's his name?"

"If I tell you, you won't have no more use for me and the Kid will shoot me."

Mad Mike thought for a moment. "All right. You got a point. You go back inside the First and Last. We'll follow you in. You tell us inside what this man's name is. We ain't going to gun down an unarmed man in front of everybody."

"Yeah," the Kid agreed. "If we want to, we can always get you later someplace quiet."

"Like if we find you haven't told us the truth," Mad Mike added.

Myles Lyman headed back toward the glowing doorway and windows of the First and Last, expecting to receive a bullet in the back at any moment. He pushed in through the batwing doors and saw the way people looked at his dust-caked clothes, at the sweat running down his gray face. Shortly afterward Mad Mike, the Kid, and Seattle Bill sidled into the saloon and stood alongside Myles at the bar.

Myles didn't waste any time. "You know that itinerant physician named Weatherbee? He's the one who organized and owns everything. I just work for him."

West of the Mississippi, every able-bodied man rose at first light, even if he did wake to find himself between clean sheets with a beautiful woman like Charlene. That didn't mean to say he couldn't go back to bed with her at some point during the day, but he rose with the sun to face the new day.

Doc Weatherbee pulled on his clothes as the early morning sun climbed high enough to stream in through the lace drapes over the windows of Charlene's cabin. He kissed her and she drowsily responded, then he firmly placed his pearl gray curly-brim derby on his head, checked himself in the mirror, and went out the door, intending to make his first stop at the barber for a shave.

A large empty freighter was passing in the street, a long wagon with high timber walls, hauled by a team of six draft horses. Doc moved to one side to escape the dust that the hooves kicked up in clouds on the morning breeze—and saw Mad Mike and Seattle Bill lurking behind a building watching him.

Doc slipped around behind the empty freighter to get to the other side of the street. The Kid was waiting on the far sidewalk, his right hand resting on his gun handle.

Doc as usual was unarmed. They were too close to him for him to make a break for it by running. He didn't know why, but he knew without doubt that these three were gunning for him. He had no place to go except one—he jumped into the empty wagon through its open back end.

He climbed up the inside of one of the high sides and peered over the edge. The Kid tore a sliver of wood with a .45 slug only a few inches from his nose. Doc got such a fright, he fell off the side and landed on his back in the wagon.

He picked up his derby, pressed it hard onto his head, and this time climbed the opposite side. The pistol shot had panicked both the driver and his horses, and now the wagon was picking up speed and lurching wildly from side to side. Doc had no time to lose. In only a few moments the three gunmen would be left behind the wagon, and they would have a clear line of sight to shoot him through its open back end.

When Doc reached the top of the freighter's high side, he saw that the vehicle was passing a substantial two-story house with a porch along its entire front. A bullet from the Kid's six-gun whizzed over his head. Another, from either Mad Mike or Seattle Bill, tickled the hairs on the back of his neck. Doc balanced for a moment on the wagon side and then leaped.

A sudden lurch helped launch him on his flight to the top of the porch fronting the two-story house. There was no shelter there, and Doc kept going—head first through a window, his derby shattering the glass and his arms protecting his face.

Doc landed on a big double bed, between a man in a nightcap and a woman in a pink nightgown. Doc looked from one to the other of them. It was Rob Lynch and his wife. The Pinkerton politely raised his hat to the lady and nodded to the gentleman.

"Damn you, Weatherbee!" Lynch snarled. The tiny man had a big .45 in his bony hand. "I'm going to blow your brains out for this!"

"What! In your wife's bed?" Doc looked shocked. "Her name will be dirt."

Rob Lynch wavered.

"No one will believe I came through the window," Doc said hurriedly. "They'll all think the worst. They always do when a husband shoots a man in bed with his wife."

Mrs. Lynch in her pink nightgown giggled. Or it might have been hysteria.

They heard scraping outside the shattered window on the porch top. It was the Kid. He had climbed up.

"Go away!" Lynch shouted.

"But we got him trapped," the Kid said, pointing his gun at Doc, who was lying back on the bed as flat and as close to Mrs. Lynch as he could.

"Not in my wife's bed!" Rob Lynch howled.

"I have to send a telegram," Doc announced.

Both men and the woman paused and looked at him.

It seemed an odd kind of statement to make at that particular moment.

CHAPTER SIX

After Raider received the telegram from Pinkerton headquarters in Chicago telling him to go to the aid of Doc Weatherbee, he spent four days almost constantly traveling—mostly by train and then by stage from Wichita—to get from northern Nevada to southwestern Kansas. By the time he arrived in Hugoton, he was exhausted, his stomach bothered him, and he wasn't done yet. There was no sign of Doc in Hugoton.

All Raider knew was that Doc must have telegraphed for help from this place. And Weatherbee was no look-alike drifter who could float into a town and out again with nobody noticing. People remembered him. Also, Hugoton was a small place, the sort of town where no one went unwatched. So Raider wasn't buying the simple story the man at the livery stables was trying to give him—that there was no Dr. Weatherbee in this town and he didn't remember none neither.

The others were out front, replacing a wheel with a cracked hub on the stage. Raider grabbed the man by the shirtfront and threw him back forcibly against the stable wall. He hooked the man's revolver from its holster, let it fall on the straw, and then cracked the man's lower lip with his knuckles. A rivulet of blood trickled over his chin.

"I don't want no lies," Raider said pleasantly. "Now think again. You remember a homeopathic doctor who probably kept his mule and wagonload of ointments here in these stables?"

"Reckon I do."

"I ain't asking about his troubles, only where he went if he ain't here."

The man wiped the blood from his mouth. "Most folk who don't get on in Hugoton move to Coronado."

"You think he went there or you know it?"

"I heard he did. They welcome anyone in that town that we don't like here."

Raider climbed back on the stage when he heard that its next stop would be Coronado. He arrived in the town about two hours later. Coronado seemed to him to look almost exactly like Hugoton—just another little cowtown, a stop-over for some on the Chisholm Trail.

"Any man run out of Hugoton is welcome in Coronado," Raider was told when he inquired after Doc.

"Yeah, I been told that already."

"He got to have some good in him someplace if they don't like him in Hugoton."

"Sure," Raider agreed patiently. "You seen Weatherbee in the last day or so?"

"I seen him fifteen minutes ago."

"Where?"

"Where he's staying. At the Bluestem Hotel. Big place

painted red down the main street. You can't miss it."

Raider headed toward the hotel, relieved to hear that his fellow Pinkerton operative seemed to be all right. So far as Raider was concerned, Doc Weatherbee was a real pain in the ass. Raider had no wish to work on assignment with him, because Doc was always making jokes at his expense and grabbing every woman in sight—no, Doc didn't have to grab them, they grabbed him and ignored Raider. No man could be expected to enjoy that.

But Weatherbee was a seasoned operative and a reliable partner, Raider would grant him that without hesitation. Yet he was a stickler for rules and regulations. In some ways Doc was even worse than Orville Huggins, with all the reports and procedures and so forth. The big difference between them was that Weatherbee knew what he was doing and Huggins didn't. Doc was safe to work with, while Orville wasn't. If Raider never saw either of them again for the rest of his life, he felt he would be missing nothing.

A Studebaker wagon pulled by a single mule left Coronado a few hours later. Canvas signs on the sides of the wagon proclaimed it to be the property of DOCTOR WEATHERBEE—HOMEOPATHIC MEDICINES—FREE CONSULTATION. Doc and Raider sat on the driver's bench, and the bottles of medicine rattled in their wooden storage boxes behind them as the wagon bumped on the rutted, uneven trail.

"You need a goddamn whip to use on this fool animal," Raider snarled about the mule. "That'd make the bitch jump."

A look of anger crossed Doc Weatherbee's face. He said nothing. He knew Raider was deliberately riling him, but he couldn't control his anger at the thought of anyone using a whip on his beloved Judith. Doc was well aware that he spoiled the mule, and that he put up with Judith's cantank-

erous moods without a word of protest. He had bought both
Judith and the wagon from a physician in Carson City and
had used the medical profession as a cover since then.

"If I had this dang stubborn animal, I'd trade her in for
a younger beast—provided I could find someone fool enough
to make the trade," Raider was saying.

As if Judith understood what Raider said, she steered the
wagon so that the front wheel on his side dropped into a
deep rut and the jolt nearly unseated him.

"You murdering spiteful critter, you oughta be put out
of pain!" Raider yelled.

Doc laughed. "Trouble is, Raider, she's too smart for
you. That mule gets the better of you every time."

It was Raider's turn to scowl silently. He always took it
seriously when Doc implied he was stupid.

To change the subject before it got dangerous, Doc said,
"There'll be hell to pay when they see this wagon roll into
Hugoton. Rob Lynch let me send a telegram, although I
doubt he really believed I'm a Pinkerton. Tom Murdock and
Jim Coulter claimed my identity papers are poor forgeries—
I wonder what Mr. Pinkerton would say to that! But Lynch
had a lingering doubt. Anyway, I owe my life to him. He
persuaded his two partners not to order me shot for organizing this bond issue, and he stopped those three loony
gunslingers from turning me into coyote food. Though I
sure thought my number was up when Jim Coulter followed
me out of town on horseback."

"You wasn't wearing a gun, I suppose," Raider said with
contempt.

"Certainly not. I can talk my way out of most situations
without having to resort to brutal, primitive methods. The
man who has to use his gun is one who doesn't know how
to use his brain."

"Thanks," Raider said, and his eyes glittered dangerously.

Doc knew from painful past experiences that Raider was highly likely to punch him out at any moment. Doc was already minus one tooth from a previous misunderstanding between him and Raider. He didn't want to lose another.

"Anyway, they ran me out of town without shooting me, and as I left, Jim Coulter rode after me. I felt sure he would try to gun me down, and I can tell you I felt mighty stupid with my revolver and shotgun in the secret compartment of the wagon. As you know, I've even got two Gatlings and sticks of dynamite down there. But I couldn't get to them and had to stay where I'm sitting now, on the driver's bench of my wagon with the reins in my hands, a sitting duck if you ever saw one."

"And this doggone mule taking her own sweet time, I'm willing to bet."

"It was a hot day and Judith was feeling the strain," Doc said crossly, confirming what Raider had guessed. "But Coulter didn't pull his gun on me. Instead he grabbed medicine bottles, uncorked them, and threw them at me. I had to stay where I was and keep moving because Mad Mike, the Kid, and Seattle Bill were hovering on the edge of town hoping for an excuse to ride after me to finish me off. Jim Coulter took advantage of this. He totally ruined my blue worsted wool suit, finest quality Boston tailoring. Fortunately my hat was knocked off early on, so it escaped. The rest of me was covered with sticky cough syrup, fish and snake oils, hair restorer, and skin balms." Doc sniffed the back of his hand. "I think I still stink of the stuff."

Raider laughed heartily—until Judith dropped the wheel nearest him in another hole and rattled his bones. Then he began to curse.

•   •   •

It was as Doc had said—as soon as the wagon was sighted nearing town, word spread and folks drifted out of the stores and saloons to see what would happen. There was not much laid on in the way of entertainment in a town the size of Hugoton, and its inhabitants knew how to make every little diversion count. Nothing like a shooting to speed up a slow afternoon.

And it looked like there was going to be some shooting. Mad Mike, Seattle Bill, and the Kid emerged from an eating house where they had been drinking coffee after double helpings of beef stew. They were sober and bored—in the mood for some action.

The three gunslingers walked together down the middle of the dusty, rutted main street till they were opposite the livery stable, where they figured—correctly as it turned out—Doc Weatherbee's wagon was headed. They saw the second man on the driver's bench with Weatherbee and guessed they should expect trouble. When the wagon came closer and they got a better look at this hombre in his black Stetson and scarred leather jacket, with his big mustache, they knew for sure there would be trouble.

Mike, Bill, and the Kid spread out to cover the wide street and block the wagon's approach. The mule hauling the wagon ambled into town at an infuriatingly slow gait, and Weatherbee tried neither to hurry nor to slow the animal. The quack seemed unconcerned, except for one thing. Today he had a gun strapped to his hip and a double-barrel shotgun on the bench beside him. They had never seen him tote a gun before.

The big mustached stranger on the bench beside him had a six-gun on his right hip and a carbine across his knees. The casual, easy way he handled the carbine told the three hired gunmen that this man knew the feel of the weapon and how to use it.

The three didn't like what they saw, but there was no backing down now. The whole town was watching them. They had run Weatherbee out of town and warned him not to come back. He had defied them. He was coming back, cool as a cucumber, facing them down in front of everyone, with this fast gun sitting beside him that he obviously reckoned could take the three of them. One thing Mike, Bill, and the Kid all agreed on was that this elegantly tailored, smooth-talking medical fake couldn't fight his way out of a paper bag. So it had to be the hombre sitting beside him.

The three gunmen were wrong about Doc Weatherbee, but their killer instinct warned them correctly about Raider. They didn't know his name, they didn't know where he had come from, but they did know that, like themselves, he lived by his gun.

Not counting Doc—and they didn't count Doc—it was three against one. No matter who this stranger was, even if he was Wild Bill Hickok himself, and he wasn't, he couldn't beat those odds if they handled things right. So they spread out across the street. That way they couldn't be wiped out by a single shotgun blast and their opponents would have to deal with bullets coming at them from three different angles.

That fool Weatherbee was bringing this upon himself. He was defying them. He was calling them down. They'd show the slick bastard and leave him bleeding in the dust.

They stiffened and their hands hovered over their gun handles when they saw Raider stand on the bench of the approaching wagon. But he was still more than a hundred yards away and their six-guns hadn't much accuracy beyond seventy-five yards, and even at that range it was skilled shooting. Only the Kid had a rifle, and he had leaned it against the wooden sidewalk next to him, wanting them to come in close so he would have a good look at their faces when they died.

Raider stepped among the wooden crates of medicine bottles till he came to a canvas-covered lump in the middle of the wagon. He ripped the canvas off and sat himself on a box behind a Gatling gun fixed to a tripod, ready to go. He fired a short burst along the tops of the false fronts on one side of the street. The bullets snapped off ornamental wooden decorations and scrollwork, which rattled down on the sidewalk planking beneath.

Then he fired a short burst just over the heads of the three gunmen confronting the wagon.

They didn't duck or take so much as one step backward.

But they didn't go for their guns neither.

"Mike, Bill, Kid, I want you to meet Raider," Doc began.

Raider cursed Doc silently for his pompous voice, and cursed Doc's mule for steadily plodding onward into six-gun range. A Gatling gun firing bullets inches above her ears was not enough to distract Judith when she sensed the nearness of a stable and a bucket of oats.

"As I told you before," Doc went on like he was a judge in a courtroom, "I am a Pinkerton operative here to scrutinize the doings of Myles Lyman. We two Pinkertons want no hassle with you three men or anyone else in this town, apart from Lyman. If you attack, we will shoot in self-defense."

Raider had to allow this speech seemed to have a good effect, and to show his own peaceful intentions, he left the Gatling gun and moved forward to sit with Doc again.

The three gunmen looked at one another.

"Hold it down, Kid," Mad Mike cautioned.

Doc was amused to see the way the aging gunman had assumed the role of wise advisor to his young fellow assassin. No doubt Mad Mike had earned his name in his younger days. However, Doc did not let his amusement show. Mad Mike had a long way to go before he would ever be called Mild Mike.

Judith recognized the livery stables and headed for them with a burst of energy.

The three gunmen stayed where they were, unmoving.

"You expect us to believe what you say about you not being Myles Lyman's boss?" Jim Coulter shouted at Doc from across the street as Doc and Raider left the Eagle Hotel. They had taken rooms there, dumped their things, and were on their way to the First and Last.

"You don't have to take my word for it, Mr. Coulter," Doc called back politely. "You can telegraph the Pinkerton National Detective Agency in Chicago, Illinois. They'll confirm what I say."

Jim Coulter aggressively crossed the street toward them. The squat cattle dealer's long arms and big hands hung down at the sides of his barrel chest, and he had an unfriendly smirk on his red fleshy face. Seattle Bill slipped out of an alley behind him and sidled along a few paces to the rear, sullen, silent, menacing.

"Lyman didn't know you were a Pinkerton on his trail before this," Coulter said. "If you haven't nailed him by this time, how do you expect to bag him now that he knows who you are?"

Doc shrugged. "I thought that once we'd convinced certain citizens in this town that he, and not me, was responsible for those bonds, matters might be taken out of our hands."

"You thought we'd do your dirty work for you?"

"I couldn't have put it better myself," Doc agreed pleasantly.

"Well, we can't," Coulter snapped.

Doc was surprised. "You're going to tolerate him in Hugoton?"

"He's skipped town. He was seen riding out toward Coronado."

Doc groaned. "I'm getting tired of running back and forth."

"It's too late now," Raider said. "We'll ride there first thing tomorrow. Where I'm going this moment is over to that saloon."

Doc went along with that suggestion.

"You!"

Doc and Raider turned about to face Seattle Bill. This was the first word Doc had ever heard the gunman speak, although he had seen him most every day for some time. But it wasn't to Doc Weatherbee that Seattle Bill had spoken. It was to Raider.

"Let's go, Bill," Jim Coulter put in authoritatively.

Bill brushed him aside with a sweep of his left hand, his eyes never leaving Raider's face, his gun hand hanging easy by his right hip.

"You ain't got no Gatling now," Seattle Bill sneered.

"I got a Remington .44, and that's all I'll be needing," Raider told him calmly.

"You ain't nothin' without a Gatling," Bill taunted him.

Raider said nothing. He just waited.

He didn't have to wait long.

With a convulsive jerk of his body, Seattle Bill went for his gun. He hauled a Starr double-action Army .44 from his holster.

Raider recognized the gun at once and guessed that his

adversary was depending on not having to cock the hammer to gain that small edge of time to come out the winner. Most professionals disliked the double-action mechanism because the extra trigger pressure needed to work it affected the aim badly. But aim was going to be no problem with the few paces that separated Seattle Bill from Raider.

It had to come down to Raider being a whole lot faster on the draw than Seattle Bill.

He was.

While Bill was raising the short barrel of the Starr Army .44 on a level with Raider's gut, the big Pinkerton whipped out his long-barrel Remington .44 and knocked back the hammer with his left hand while he was still raising the gun, an instant before he squeezed the trigger.

Raider hadn't had time to level the gun properly, and the flying bullet hit Seattle Bill inside the left hip, shattering the pelvic bone and dropping him as a useless cripple.

But Bill never was to live to see life as an invalid, since Raider followed his first shot with a second, without pausing to see where the first bullet hit but knowing it was likely to miss altogether because his aim had not been true. The first bullet had not missed, and neither did the second. The speeding lead projectile tore into Bill's lower chest as he was collapsing from the first bullet's impact.

He lay on his back on the street, gasping, with blood spurting from his chest wound.

Raider gave Jim Coulter a hard stare and holstered his smoking iron.

"I'll tell Mike and the Kid it wasn't your fault," Coulter volunteered. "Bill went against my orders."

Doc nodded toward Seattle Bill, sprawled in the roadway. "Better not to move him. He'll die more comfortably the way he is. It won't be long now."

"I hear you owe Doc Weatherbee for some medicine and a suit," Raider said to Coulter.

"Sure thing," Coulter said, reaching into his pocket as he walked around Bill, who was now moaning his last, and handed five twenty-dollar gold pieces to Doc. "A hundred bucks more than covers it."

Doc took the money.

Raider said thoughtfully, "I reckon it must be worth near a hundred bucks just to see Weatherbee smeared with his own medicines."

"Sure I been involved in questionable land deals," Myles Lyman said to the town councilmen in Coronado. "That's what makes me ideal for your situation. The fight between Coronado and Hugoton is under the table. What better man could you have working for you than a real estate swindler?" He preened in his riverboat gambler's outfit and pushed back his gray hair. "They hire gunmen, you hire gunmen. But hired guns are dumb—they can take you only so far. Here's your big chance to hire brains. Plus I got a grudge to settle with Murdock, Coulter, and Lynch for wrecking my bond issue for Smallwood in Comanche County."

"What's happening with those bonds?" one man asked. "I was thinking of buying some myself."

"Don't," Myles said. "They're worthless. Murdock and those others killed one salesman and scared off the others. That bond issue is dead while those sidewinders are still alive—or at least while they still control Hugoton. So I'm not being underhanded with you. Straight and aboveboard, I want to get back at them Hugoton varmints that spoiled my bond issue, and I reckon my best way to do that is to throw in my lot with you boys and give my best to Coronado."

"Makes sense," one councilman muttered.

"Course, since I don't stand nothing to gain," Myles went on, "'tis only reasonable I get something from the town to defray my expenses, along with a free room at the Bluestem Hotel, some meals, and maybe a few drinks as well, to show there's good feeling."

"He'll be asking for women and horses next," one councilman said sarcastically.

"Them too," Myles said with a grin. "Women and horses."

They were burying Seattle Bill on Boots Row in the graveyard as Doc and Raider rode out of Hugoton next morning. They had kept their rooms at the Eagle Hotel and left Judith and the wagon in the livery stables. Hugoton was better equipped than Coronado in places to stay and eat and drink, according to Doc. Raider was unaware that Doc's real reason for wanting to return to Hugoton was Charlene. They rode on two hired horses, both badly broken and in need of strong handling, but big powerful animals that would bear up well to hard riding.

They cantered across the level land, thick with buffalo grass, toward a ridge of very low hills that was about midway between Hugoton and Coronado.

"What're we going to do to Lyman when we find him?" Raider asked.

"Damned if I know," Doc replied. "Let's just make sure he's settled in there. I hope the money those Cleveland investors paid as their Pinkerton fee runs out soon. Following con men around from town to town with no evidence to lay a finger on them is not the sort of work I enjoy."

"Maybe I'll just shoot him and get it over with," Raider offered with a straight face.

"I know that had to be a joke," Doc snapped. He was

almost certain that sooner or later this would happen in any case. Even Allan Pinkerton, Doc had heard, felt called upon to warn prospective clients of the damage Raider was likely to cause if assigned to their case.

Doc was not in the best of moods, what with this ferrying back and forth between the two towns and this being the second day in a row he was wearing a revolver on his hip and keeping a shotgun by his side. Doc often went for months on end without toting a gun. But when a genuine need arose to carry a weapon, he grudgingly did so. It did nothing to improve his mood.

The sun was climbing higher over their heads, and they could feel the heat increasing by the minute as they rode.

"We'll get to Coronado before it becomes really hot," Doc told Raider. "We can stay there till late afternoon, when things cool off."

Both men had weathered hot sun many times before, and they respected it—by keeping out of it unless they really had to trek beneath the full onslaught of its merciless rays.

They crossed the ridge of low hills and continued across the grassy plain toward Coronado in the distance.

No one ever took a Kansas cowtown by surprise in broad daylight. Riders approaching could be seen over the nearly level sea of grass while they were still miles away. The riders, in their turn, felt exposed and vulnerable to hidden eyes and hidden guns as they neared the cluster of low timber buildings that made up the usual cowtown. Raider and Doc were no exceptions. Their experiences as Pinkerton operatives had honed sharp their sense of impending trouble. Neither one said anything to the other, but both had grown silent and edgy and watchful.

Raider finally said very casually, "Don't seem to be much moving in the town for this time of day."

"I was thinking the same myself," Doc confirmed.

They let it go at that. The town was unnaturally quiet, which could mean just about anything or nothing. The two had worked together often enough to trust each other and to hang back and let things happen.

And things did happen. The first thing that happened was a rifle bullet that sailed between them at about chest level.

"Ain't no turning back now," Raider said calmly.

"Quickest way to get shot in the back," Doc agreed, and they both rode unflinchingly onward to Coronado.

"Right now I sure as hell feel like a green bottle sitting on a wall," Raider grumbled.

"You being the larger of us, I reckon if they decide to plug one of us, they'll go for you as the easier target."

"Unless they hate the sight of eastern city dudes so much they go for the smaller target."

Doc grinned. "I hadn't thought of that."

Another bullet tore through the air between them, making a sound like a crazed hornet.

"I guess if they was going to shoot us, they'd have done it by now," Raider judged, and they rode on.

No more shots were fired. Instead nine or ten men climbed off the bars of a corral and looked expectantly at them. Half of them carried rifles—any one or two of them could have fired the shots.

Doc and Raider pulled up their horses about ten yards off. Doc called to them, "You men trying to tell us something with those two bullets?"

"Sure," one of them answered. "Turn around and go back to Scumville."

"Where's that?"

"Scumville's what we call Hugoton around here."

"I see," Doc said. "Well, that's none of our concern.

We're not interested in any quarrels between your towns. Now, as for firing bullets at us, that's not a good idea, in case you might hit us. And if a bunch of you boys take to shooting Pinkertons who aren't doing you any harm, you could be bringing down a whole lot of National Detective Agency trouble on yourselves and this town. That clear?"

"Scumville hired you Pinkertons to spy on us," one man shouted.

Doc looked indignant. "It's against Pinkerton rules to get involved in land wars and the kind of troubles you people have with Hugoton. Mr. Pinkerton would never permit his operatives—"

"Mr. Pinkerton, my ass!" one shouted.

"Let him come to Coronado. We'll take care of him!" another yelled.

Doc was firm. "We have one interest here as Pinkerton operatives. That's Myles Lyman. Not you. And not Hugoton."

"How come you haven't arrested Lyman before this?" one asked.

Doc hesitated. The man had found his weak point. "We're still gathering evidence."

"Sounds to me like you're harassing Lyman," this man went on. "Way you're following him around trying to stir up trouble for him don't strike me as strictly legal."

"We're not trying to stir up trouble for Myles Lyman," Doc said. "He can't help but stir it up himself. We just have to wait."

"Well, you ain't waiting here in Coronado. Who's that big lug?" The man pointed at Raider. "Don't he have a tongue in his head?"

Raider growled, "Leave me out of your talk, you flat-heeled peeler."

The townsman saw he had gone too far, didn't dare trade insults with this big hombre in black, and got real quiet.

At that moment Myles Lyman swaggered from behind a building, where he had obviously been observing what was going on. His eyes were glazed and red-rimmed, his face gray and ravaged by lines of fatigue. When he spoke his voice was thick, and it was plain that he was holding a gutful of booze.

"Why're you talking with those two? I warned you men they'd come here pretending to follow me. That's their cover while they work for Murdock, Coulter, and Lynch. Hugoton's hired them. Why do you think they let Weatherbee go back there after he'd come here? They haven't let no other man do it. Why him? Because he made a deal with them, that's why! He's going to do you in if you let him!"

Lyman grabbed a rifle from the man next to him and shot from the hip at Doc. He took everyone by surprise, including Raider, because at first he seemed too far gone to be able to do this. Raider had allowed some of the crowd of men to get between him and Lyman, so now he couldn't lay a bullet on him.

Doc's horse went down beneath him. Doc jumped clear, and then all of a sudden one or two of the others were shooting also. Weatherbee rolled behind the carcass of his mount, lying on its side and still kicking, to duck out of the way of the bullets.

Raider spurred his horse, cutting between the crowd of men and Doc. He hid down the far side of the horse from them, Indian-style, hanging from the crook of one knee in the saddle and clinging to the horse's neck. He emptied his revolver into them from beneath his horse's head and saw two or three of them drop. Then he felt his horse stumble, knew the animal was hit, and threw himself clear. The weight of a horse crashing down on a man can splinter his strongest bones.

Having hung on to his Remington handgun as he hit the dirt, Raider got to his knees and waited for the dust and his head to clear.

There were three crumpled forms on the ground before him. Lyman and the others had retreated behind a building and were sniping at them, while Doc returned their fire from behind the body of his downed horse.

Raider first reloaded his revolver, holstered it, then hauled his Model 94 Winchester carbine from the saddle sheath of his injured horse. He worked the lever action of the .30-.30 carbine and put a bullet in his horse's forehead to ease its miseries. Next he ran for cover behind a corner of the corral.

Wood was scarce and valuable on the Kansas prairies, and this corral was constructed not of the tapering trunks of pine trees but of any old bits and pieces of discarded lumber that could be nailed or wired together to pen horses in. These odds and ends provided good cover for Raider, and he pinned the townsmen behind the building with his carbine while Doc loosed his saddle and bridle from his dead horse and carried them to the corral. Then he fetched the gear from Raider's horse while Raider showed Lyman and the others he meant business by catching one man in the left upper arm when he tried to line up a long gun on him from the cover of the building. The injured man was hooting and hollering, rolling about on the ground in the open, plucking at his arm like a maniac. Raider could've sent a bullet up his left nostril, but instead he held off and even held his fire when a rifle with a white handkerchief tied to the barrel was waved from behind the building and two unarmed men came out to grab the wounded man and haul him off for medical care.

Doc got two mounts saddled in the corral. Raider pulled back some wooden poles and grabbed the reins of the second horse as Doc rode through the gap on the first. After sending two more bullets bouncing off the side of the house behind which the townsmen were hiding, Raider mounted up and cantered after Doc. They both rode low in the saddle and spurred their horses so they would kick up dust and conceal their outlines from the riflemen behind.

Bullets whistled after them, but none came even near. Their horses were fresh and strong, and they made good time toward the ridge of low hills between Coronado and Hugoton.

Doc waved at Raider and pointed behind them. Maybe a score of horsemen followed them. The posse had not gained on them as they reached the spine of low hills and saw Hugoton away across the prairie grass.

CHAPTER SEVEN

Things had gotten tight in Colorado for Turk Calhoun. The wanted posters were offering $5,000 for him, dead or alive. The money was put up by railroads and banks who were good for it, and bounty hunters had begun to move in. No matter how mean and well protected a badman thinks he is, he's never safe from professional bounty hunters when the money is good. Turk Calhoun had once been a bounty hunter himself and had competed with the best of them for a chance to take badmen who believed themselves almost unconquerable. The plain facts tended to be that bounty hunters were meaner, smarter, and hungrier than successful badmen sitting back and enjoying their ill-gotten gains. Turk had had a close call, and now he was the one who was going to pull the surprise—by disappearing. By the time word got back that he was now operating in Kansas, the bounty hunters would have moved somewhere else, and the Colorado banks and railroads would not be so willing to pay a reward for someone raising hell in another state.

Turk and his men crossed the state line a little after dawn and followed the Arkansas River east toward Dodge City, still three days' ride away. They took it easy through the rich grasslands and stopped to look at a huge herd of buffalo grazing contentedly. The herd stretched maybe two miles long and a half mile wide, the animals thick together and shouldering each other for room, like an enormous swarm of huge bees.

"Don't see herds like this so often anymore," one of the men remarked. "Only a few years back, you'd see herds all over that'd make even this one look small."

Turk was less interested in such things than he was in killing and butchering one of the animals. "Let's try to pick ourselves out a cow or calf—them bulls is tougher than leather. Take care to let them see us coming slow at 'em, so they don't take sudden fright. I sure don't want to be stomped to hell if they come this way, and they're dumb enough to do that if we give them a fright."

The six riders spread out and advanced in a line, their only plan being to get close enough for a rifle shot at a single beast. But though they eased forward, their horses walking so slowly they had time to pause and nibble the rich grass, the buffalo herd grew increasingly agitated before they got anywhere close to it.

Then they saw the reason why. Four Indian riders circled around from behind the herd, traveling fast on their ponies and shooting with rifles at animals at the edge of the herd. As the buffaloes stampeded away from them, another wave of Indian riders came out of nowhere and cut down more of the animals.

Turk didn't have to say a word to his men. He headed for the river, and his men along with him.

One said, "Comanches! Goddamn, I hate them critters!"

"Not half as much as they hate you," Turk snarled. "If you value your skin, you'll stick close to the water and hope we cross it before they decide to go after our meat instead of the buffalo."

"Maybe they ain't seen us."

Turk Calhoun laughed, baring his stained yellow teeth. "There's nothing bigger than a prairie dog that them Comanches miss seeing. You ask me, I think they're playing a game with us."

"Cat and mouse?" a thin tubercular youth asked. He was dressed like an out-of-work bank clerk, down-at-heel but still straining for respectability. He couldn't have been more than eighteen, and his age and appearance contrasted strongly with those of the others, all more than ten years older than he and as windblown and tattered as old tumbleweed.

"Cat and mouse," Calhoun confirmed. He was gaunt and big-boned, and had an air of command about him befitting the high-level officer he had once been in the Confederate army. "'Cept we ain't no mouse, and there ain't no cat in this land mean and fast as your regular Comanche. Unless we get in that river fast, they're going to swoop down on us like you just seen them do to those buffalo. But hold your horses there—don't seem in no hurry. There's no way we can reach that water if they want to cut us off, and one sure way to make them want to do that is to let them see you turn tail and run."

Turk Calhoun had surrounded himself with good men, knowing it took only a single weak link for the chain to break. Not one panicked and broke for the river. Not one even looked fearfully across at the Indians driving the buffalo this way and that, picking off animals that slowed in bewilderment.

"Must be forty braves," one man commented.

"And if they're killing this many buffalo, they must have

a big encampment not too far way, maybe somewhere along the river," the tubercular youth reasoned. "I think they're too busy putting meat aside to bother about us."

Turk laughed. "That's white-man thinking you're doing, Snead. Go easy and put by something for tomorrow, like the Good Book says. 'Cept Comanches don't go along with that. I tell you the only reason they're going on playing with them buffalo is to tempt us to make a break for it. They want to see us try to hightail it out of here before they come down on us. What I want them to see is that we're giving them respect and not disturbing them—but we ain't bowing our heads. Got that?"

The small group of riders rode steadily for the wide Arkansas waters, and the Indians, no more than a mile away on the level grassland, continued harrying the buffalo herd into short confused charges that were always cut off by more riders approaching from the opposite direction. A naive stranger might have supposed the Comanches were so engrossed in their task that they hadn't noticed the six horsemen slipping off toward the big river.

Calhoun knew they would never make it, but he wasn't letting the others know that. Except for Snead. Once the sickly youth fastened on something, he bit through to the bone. Snead gave him an arrogant glance to show he knew what was in Calhoun's mind and was no more fearful than he. To see the cold courage of a fighting man in such an unlikely person intrigued Calhoun. He had seen it before in high-born Southern gentlemen who had died next to him on the battlefields, too proud to cringe, who had departed this life with a disdainful smile on their lips. Snead was no high-born gentleman, any more than he, Turk Calhoun, was. But they were both Southerners to the bone. Calhoun was inclined to think that was it.

They were coming at them! With lightning speed and at

some secret signal, all at once the Comanche warriors detached themselves from the buffalo herd and urged their bareback ponies across the intervening grassland, waving their rifles and whooping scarifying war cries. This was it! Turk and his men had no chance in hell of getting to the riverbank. They were six men caught out in the open on six weary horses with nothing more than knee-high buffalo grass to hide in.

The wave of Comanche warriors bore down on them, a hunting party of more than forty braves, traveling light on agile ponies.

"Get in a knot!" Calhoun was yelling. "Every man face into them! Fire at will!"

And they did. But the Comanches crouched low on their horses' necks. Even when Turk and his men brought down their ponies, the warriors charged onward on foot behind those still mounted. Every one of the six emptied the seventeen rounds in their Winchester repeating rifles before the Indians reached them, and then they drew their .45 Peacemakers to loose off their last shots so they could die like men with their boots on.

Clouds of blue gunsmoke mixed into the swirls of red dust as the Comanches hit the six riders, the way an eagle swoops down and snaps the back of a prairie dog caught in the open. No more than the rodent's teeth and claws could beat off the talons and great curved beak, no more chance than that had Turk and his men.

After the wave of Comanches broke over the six stationary riders, none were left on their horses. Calhoun and Snead found themselves standing side by side, unhurt, while their four companions lay dead or injured near them. The Peacemaker had been knocked from Snead's grip, and he stood now with his hands empty. Calhoun's pistol was jammed. He shook it, tried to revolve the barrel, cursed, and threw it down. The Indian riders wheeled around for another charge, and the Comanches on foot were just reaching them.

Calhoun drew his fourteen-inch bowie. Likewise Snead drew one with a ten-inch blade. They stood back to back as the Comanches on foot circled them and those on horseback looked on. The warriors near them put away their rifles and revolvers and drew long, wicked-looking blades. They wore only a single eagle feather in their long black hair. A few were lightly painted; most were not at all. Theirs had been only a hunting party, unprepared for war—if it can be said that a Comanche is ever unprepared for war.

Turk Calhoun had spent each day never knowing if it would be his last and ready at all times to fight to the death. He'd begun to live like this in the War Between the States, and he'd lived this way ever since, always aware that one of these days—it had to be close by now—was the one with his death notice attached.

Still, he felt no sorrow, no regret, standing back to back with Snead, parrying the knife thrusts of the circling, shouting Comanches. Then they eased up in order to let the two see what was happening to their injured and dead companions. Some of the warriors stood above their prone bodies, cut a circle below the hairline, and peeled off the scalp, leaving a raw fleshy bleeding knob. Thornton screamed and struggled as they tore the skin from the top of his head. The three others were dead or at least gave no sign of feeling anything. Herman was almost bald, with only a band of hair from ear to ear above the back of his neck. The Comanches had little use for his nearly bare scalp and tossed it from one to the other, joking and laughing.

The Indians had plainly hoped to strike fear or heartbreak

into Calhoun and Snead by this display, but they failed because neither man gave one sweet damn what happened to these four and had no intention of living through it himself. But the Comanches seemed to assume that the four were close to them like fellow tribesmen. They pointed at the two men's heads and held up their long sharp blades. Then the warriors began to close in for real.

Snead took the first wound—the tip of a blade high in his chest. Instead of weakening him, the injury seemed to turn the sickly youth meaner, more like a caged rat. A few knife cuts in Calhoun's leathery skin made no difference one way or the other to him. The more the two were goaded, the better they fought back—they even inflicted as many cuts as they took themselves, outnumbered as they were.

One of the mounted Indians spoke, and suddenly the warriors stopped driving at them with their blades, stopped circling them, stopped shouting. The Comanches just stood and stared at the two amazed white men, standing back to back, slashed and bleeding, but still holding their bowies in front of them.

The mounted Indian spoke again, this time at length. Finally he pointed to one of the other mounted Indians, and this warrior looked at Calhoun and Snead.

"Our war chief says it is not often we meet brave men, and we have no wish to harm men who show courage as you have done. You may go, and we will give you horses. Or you may join with us and we will give each of you an honored place in our band, a good woman, horses, and weapons."

Calhoun and Snead were dumbstruck.

"Do you understand what I said?" the mounted Indian said in better English than either Calhoun or Snead spoke, but curiously careful, like a well-educated foreigner might speak the language.

Ever the Southerner, Calhoun responded warily, "You have more than a tetch of Alabama in that accent of yours."

Snead elbowed him. "That Injun's a white, same as you and me!"

Turk looked. "Sure as cotton, you're an Alabama boy gone savage!"

The mounted man smiled. "The Comanches took me when I was a boy. I'm more Comanche now than the Comanches themselves."

"That's your business, boy," Turk snapped, once more himself. "What's that you say about letting us go and giving us horses?"

"You can go. Or join with us."

"We want to go," Calhoun said.

Some Indians rode up with spare horses on long lines. Most were the small fast ponies the Indians favored, but some were large mounts. Turk and Snead saddled up two of these.

"Can we take our guns?" Turk asked.

The white-turned-Comanche nodded.

Turk made sure to take one of the other pistols and leave his jammed Peacemaker behind.

Then the war chief began to talk at length again.

Turk Calhoun searched his eyes while he talked to see if he had changed his mind.

"Our war chief says you must not go farther east along the river. You must go north or south or back the way you came."

"We'll head south," Turk offered.

They nodded their respect to the war chief and headed for the Arkansas, looking for a place to ford it or a neck of smooth water to swim their horses across.

"What's down this way?" Snead asked.

"Nothing but grass and after that the Indian Territory.

We'll head south till we hit the Chisholm Trail. There's some small towns down there that might have our kind of action after we find ourselves a few new men."

"Can you get over them Injuns letting us go like that?"

Turk Calhoun laughed. "You just can never tell with them Comanches."

Doc and Raider were surprised to find the First and Last saloon shut up.

A man directed them. "Go across the street and try the new place, the Setting Sun. It's their opening day today."

They recognized the man as a part-time barkeep at the First and Last and wondered why he was directing them to the competition. Inside the Setting Sun they found Murdock and Coulter buying drinks for friends at the bar. The Pinkertons had learned that these two, along with Lynch, had recently taken over the ownership of the First and Last, plus a lot of other things in the town of Hugoton.

Doc talked to the owner of the new saloon, and he seemed puzzled as to why First and Last had closed its doors for his opening night and why the competition was patronizing his place. He hadn't had a lot of capital to lay in much booze. His stock was already running low. In order to attract customers, he was giving drinks on credit to those he knew. The atmosphere was getting crazier.

By the time the two Pinkertons left, the hard liquor had run out, the mirrors and windows were smashed, and chairs were hitting the walls. The roughnecks were finishing the last kegs of beer and some jugs of blackberry wine.

Once they were outside the door, Raider said, "It's going to take a month for them before they can fix this place up and open again for business."

Doc shrugged. "The Setting Sun won't be opening again.

But you'll see tomorrow that the First and Last will."

Raider assumed Doc was heading for Charlene's house. He had met her and liked her. While Doc was preoccupied with her, Raider knew he wouldn't be subjected to Doc's jeers and jokes to pass the time. For the truth was, they were both idle. And they had nothing to do all day in a small town where there was little to distract an idle man. Normally Doc would have tormented Raider to amuse himself. Raider was more than willing now to walk him toward her cabin, where she could distract him.

But Doc still had time to get in a dig. "I liked the way the marshal warned you personally never to break the law in this town."

A vein in Raider's forehead throbbed with rage. "Yellabelly bastard! Ever since they made Mad Mike town marshall, he's been sniveling around looking for a weak point in me. And that murdering rat they call the Kid, imagine him a deputy marshal!"

"I think you're going to have to watch out you don't break the law, Raider, now that you gunned down their buddy, Seattle Bill. I think those boys might rough you up a little if they got you in a jail cell."

"Hell, them little ants couldn't pinch me without their guns—and their trouble with guns is I'm faster than either one of 'em."

Doc shook his head doubtfully. "I just don't know, Raider. I'm getting kind of worried about your safety in this town. Maybe I should ask Chicago for more operatives. The way I see it, their added salaries would use up the fee faster, and we'd be out of here sooner."

Raider shook his head violently. "I don't need no additional Pinkertons down here."

He hadn't told Doc about Orville Huggins. Weatherbee

was bad enough. Weatherbee *and* Huggins would bring him to his knees faster than Mad Mike and the Kid ever could.

Myles Lyman was trying to raise cash. He had no lack of his own money, of course, but to Myles, raising cash always meant other people's. That was one of his business rules—risk other people's money, never your own. He was seeing things clear in Coronado. Myles had stayed long enough in Hugoton to see how Lynch, Coulter, and Murdock had taken over the town, so if Hugoton ever did grab the cattle trade from Wichita and Dodge City, those three men would be the ones who would chiefly benefit. To the tune of millions of dollars. Murdock's game made all of Myles's real estate efforts look small time in comparison. Hell, if a turkey like Murdock could take over in Hugoton, a genius like himself should have no trouble in Coronado.

But first he had to raise cash to buy cattle. Set up Coronado as a stock-buying town the way Hugoton had already done. Myles himself knew nothing about livestock, but so far as he could figure, that wouldn't matter. He'd buy the longhorns driven up from Texas at a dollar a head, graze them to one of those government agents with franchises to feed reservation Indians. Sometimes the herd could be sold, stampeded, and sold for the second time next day to the same agent. Or a herd of 2,000 animals could magically become one of 4,000, with Myles and the agent splitting the government money paid for the nonexistent animals meant to feed no-account Indians anyway. Myles figured he could come up with some fresh schemes also that no one else had thought of before. What he needed was to raise money to buy those first herds.

Myles also needed someone who could get those two Pinkertons off his back. He'd been a fool at first in never guessing that Weatherbee was a Pinkerton and interested in his doings. Myles was afraid of Raider. News had reached him of Raider's killing of Seattle Bill. He figured that Mad Mike and the Kid would settle that score with Raider sooner or later. In the meantime he needed to be safe to move around outside the town of Coronado. The Pinkertons couldn't come into Coronado after him anymore, now that murder warrants were sworn out against them for the three men they had killed before being chased back to Hugoton by the posse.

But folks since then had seen Raider and Weatherbee riding close by, as though they feared nothing. Myles had no idea what they might do to him if they ran into him away from Coronado, and he didn't want to find out. But neither could he complete his plans for taking over Coronado and becoming a cattle millionaire like Murdock and the others if he was scared to leave town.

Myles Lyman sat and cogitated on these problems with no impatience or annoyance. He would find solutions for them, and when the rewards were this big—greater by far than he had ever tried to achieve previously—the work was a pleasure to do.

Turk Calhoun had already won a bundle. He played the roulette wheel and he won. He played faro and draw and stud poker and he won and won. He drank so much expensive Tennessee bourbon he could hardly talk anymore— and he still won.

"Ain't no man in this town can sit down with me and beat me," Turk boasted, gazing around the gaming room.

Players scowled at him, but none took up his challenge. He was on a run, and he was the kind of man who would milk a good run for all it was worth. And he enjoyed success. Calhoun had been familiar enough with loss all his life not to enjoy success when it came to him in any form.

"To hell with your green faces of envy!" he shouted. "Not one of you is man enough to match me!"

He pointed at one gambler who looked a bit ridiculous in his fancy pearl-button vest because of his gray hair and lined face. "You got the experience, Pop! Want to try your hand?"

Myles Lyman shook his head. "You're no spring chicken yourself. But no, I won't play you. Not that I'm afraid—but cards, dice, and so forth are not what I care to gamble on."

"What do you play on, then?" Calhoun asked, curious now about this man.

"Perhaps we'll talk about it tomorrow. After you lose back all the money you've won today."

Turk laughed. "True enough, friend." He waved the greenbacks and rattled gold coins. "Easy come, easy go. Money don't tame a man like me. Neither does the lack of it."

While another man might have guarded his winnings, the Southerner seemed to care nothing for any threat the others in the Plain Hell saloon might offer to his newfound riches. This, in a kind of way, was taken as a general insult, besides the needling way he had of suggesting no one in Coronado had the guts to gamble against him anymore—and this being true only put a more bitter edge on things.

When the Southern stranger who called himself Turk seemed far gone and was no longer bothering to pick up gold coins that slipped through his fingers onto the floor, five cowhands on their way back to Texas after a drive to Dodge City—cowhands who had blown in Coronado the last few dollars they hadn't spent up in Dodge, and had only a hungry trip back to look forward to and months of lonely riding on the range before they had the cash for a blast again—these five saw two more weeks of hell-raising in the dollars that Turk had won.

They drifted easy and casual toward him, knowing him for a fighting man and maybe a skilled gunslinger. Five on one, no matter how good he was—they had him nailed, and his money was theirs.

"You cheated us out of that money you got there, mister," one of the cowhands told Turk.

"Better give it all back to us if you don't want trouble," another added.

Turk laughed at them. "Why, you penniless bums weren't even playing in any game with me. You don't hardnose me. Time you boys was heading back down to Texas and finding yourselves a job instead of interfering with your betters up in these parts."

"We don't want no trouble with you, mister. You just give us that money and you see this here fist—"

A shot rang out. The cowhand talking doubled over clutching his gut and toppled to the floor.

A curl of blue smoke rose from the muzzle of Turk Calhoun's Peacemaker, and the four other cowhands were slapping leather. There was no way now Turk could gun all four—one, maybe two at the most—before he had to eat lead himself.

Four rapid shots cracked from the door, and the cowhands all went down like skittles.

Myles Lyman stood to look. He had hardly noticed the consumptive young man in the greasy suit who had nursed a glass of gin all night, leaning near the door. Myles looked now at the expert way his small hands worked the big Colt .45 Peacemaker as he removed the spent shells and slipped four new shells in the chambers.

"You won't gamble with me, and you *can't* rob me!" Turk Calhoun was bellowing. "Me and Snead here, we'll take on this whole fucking town! We'll kill the lot of you!"

"Calm down, gentlemen, calm down," Myles said, stepping over two of the dead cowhands on his way to the bar. "Let me buy you both a drink. I think you two are going to be a very valuable addition to this town."

CHAPTER EIGHT

As soon as he arrived back in Hugoton from Wichita, Rob Lynch got together with Tom Murdock and Jim Coulter at the First and Last saloon, open once again across the street from the boarded-up, half-wrecked, and permanently closed Setting Sun. His news was not good.

"Of course I double-checked and made sure," he told Tom Murdock irritably. "The Missouri Pacific Railroad say they're going to keep on course for Coronado and will beat the Santa Fe Railroad in their race to Hugoton. I offered them everything we could deliver—plus a few things we couldn't—if they'd race the Santa Fe to Hugoton instead, but they wouldn't hear of it. In fact they made some snooty remarks about how Hugoton had fallen into the hands of what they called undesirable elements. They also hinted broadly that they held me and my associates responsible for some of the difficulties their survey engineers and track-laying crews have been having. One company man—a New

Englander with a bushy beard—went so far as to say that the railroad might not be above retaliating against those they considered responsible for any future major difficulties."

Murdock muttered curses under his breath. "I suppose we've gone as far as we dare in interfering with the rails. Those railroaders ain't pushovers, not when you get them riled up at you."

"And the railroads have the federal government behind them in everything they want to do," Lynch added. "As you say, Tom, we gotta go easy on them. What I say is we make it so Coronado is not a place they want to be."

"How?" Coulter asked.

"Only way is level that town to the ground," Murdock growled.

"Maybe," Lynch countered. "Maybe not."

"What do you mean?" Murdock demanded.

"How do I know what I mean? Let me think. You might try thinking yourself for a change, instead of always trying to pick my brain."

The three men, natural rivals, were stuck with one another and they knew it. If they disliked each other before, they hated each other now on closer contact. Each was convinced the other two were clinging to him as useless bloodsucking parasites. The only trust they shared was that the misfortune or injury of one was the misfortune or injury of all.

They glowered over their drinks in silence at their table in the First and Last, oblivious to the high jinks and crude laughter all about them as drovers, cowhands, drifters, gamblers, and whores raucously went about their pleasures and businesses.

Something caught Jim Coulter's eye. It was Charlene. She was sitting at a table on the far side of the crowded saloon, so that he had not noticed her before. Two men were at her table—Weatherbee and Raider.

"Those goddamn Pinkertons oughta be run outa here," Coulter grumbled.

Murdock laughed. "You going to do it on your own, Jim?"

Lynch, ever looking for the edge, said, "No. Like we agreed before, we leave them here because they're good for us. They're out to get Lyman, and that puts them on our side."

"But we already took care of Lyman," Coulter blurted out, louder than he intended. He lowered his voice. "There ain't a marketer between here and New York who will touch his goddamn bonds after what happened in Topeka."

"That's not what I'm talking about," Lynch said.

Murdock was suddenly interested. "Rob, you think there's truth behind the talk that Lyman is setting hisself up agin us in Coronado?"

"Sure I do," Lynch told him, and both became so involved in this discussion that they paid no heed to Coulter as he swallowed down a couple of drinks, one after the other, pushed back his chair, and headed across the floor of the packed saloon.

Doc said a few words to Raider when he saw him coming.

"He one of your admirers, Charlene?" Raider asked.

"Just because I said no to Jim makes him want what he can't have." Charlene tossed her long hair over one bare shoulder. "The longer he can't have, the more he wants."

"He doesn't look to me like he's enjoying it much," Raider said as Coulter neared their table.

The cattleman stood there, and when neither Doc nor Raider extended him an invitation to join them, he ignored them and talked to Charlene like he and she were alone. He told her she looked real good. She thanked him. He wanted to buy her dinner. She wasn't hungry. How about the best French champagne? She wasn't thirsty. He wanted to talk with her. She didn't have time to listen.

"Well, you seem to have time enough to throw away on no-good layabouts," Jim Coulter said, turning from sweet to sour.

"My time is my own, Jim. I spend it how I please."

"Maybe not while you're in Hugoton, you don't," he sneered. "Maybe here you better listen good when certain people speak to you."

This was too much for Raider. "That ain't no way to talk to a lady when I'm about."

Coulter paid him no attention. He waved his finger in Charlene's face. "Enough is enough. You've had your fun and games with me. That's all over now. You and me are leaving here to have ourselves a talk."

"I don't want to! Save me, Doc!"

Weatherbee first had to calm Raider, who wanted to settle this thing with his gun. By this time Coulter had grabbed Charlene by the arm. Doc hit him on the mouth with his fist. Coulter was knocked on his ass. As he climbed to his feet, he heard the sniggers of the locals.

"I'll get you for setting this up, you bitch," he snarled at Charlene. He stared at Doc, mean as a polecat, and his hand hovered near his gun. As usual Doc was unarmed. Then Coulter glanced fast at Raider and saw the big Remington on his hip. Coulter made a show of unbuckling his gunbelt and placing it and his weapon on a nearby table, where he told the customers in a joking confident way, "Watch me whup this eastern dandy."

Doc Weatherbee was waiting for him, his suit coat perfectly tailored, boots polished, silk vest sporting green diamonds on a canary background, his pearl gray derby correctly brushed and at a fashionable tilt on his head. He didn't seem in the least disturbed by the prospect of fisticuffs with Jim Coulter.

"That was a sucker punch you caught me with, you sneaking sidewinder," Coulter yelled as he came at Weatherbee.

The cattle dealer threw a haymaker at the Pinkerton, who effortlessly sidestepped it and delivered a body blow in return that made Coulter look like he had bit on a lemon.

"You have the luck of the devil," he gasped and came at Doc again, this time trying a straight right in Doc's face.

Doc stopped the blow with his left hand, brushed aside a second straight right, and hammered home an uppercut that lifted Coulter off his feet and sent him in under a table.

Having dusted off his sleeves and straightened his hat, Doc Weatherbee made a dignified exit with Charlene on his arm. Raider stayed behind to kill the bottle of whiskey. And Jim Coulter's legs were stirring but he still hadn't come out from under the table.

"It ain't even sundown yet, Doc," Charlene said, giggling. "What're the neighbors going to think?"

"First time I've seen you concerned about that. And I guess most of the neighbors you have here plain won't give a damn, and those that do will only be wishing they were in my place."

"Like Jim Coulter?"

"Just so long as they don't get as pushy about it as him, it makes no matter to me," Doc told her.

"It makes a girl feel funny all over to have two men fighting over her. I want to thank you, Doc, for standing up for me."

"I always stand up for you, Charlene."

"I don't mean in bed. I mean the way you knocked out

Jim. It's been coming to him a long time. Women tell me he gets real mean with them and bats them about."

"You're going to have to watch yourself with him from now on in. He'll be waiting for a chance to get at you when my back is turned."

"I know," she said. When they got inside her place and closed the door behind them, she threw her arms around his neck and kissed him. "It was so great to see you fight on account of me, Doc. I tell you it's got me tingling all over."

"I hope you're not going to depend on me to do it every day to get you excited," Doc said with a smile. "You might be nursing my injuries as often as making love with me."

But Charlene wasn't interested in further discussion. She came at him in a rush, knocked him on his back onto her big bed, and pinned his body down with her legs and hands.

"It might be easier if we took our clothes off," Doc suggested, ever mindful of the creases being inflicted on his jacket and a possible dent in his hat.

Charlene relented only long enough to practically tear off her own clothes, and Doc hurriedly got out of his before she could rip them from his body. They stood in their bare skins for a moment, avidly admiring each other's parts, then she rushed him again, intending to push him backward onto the bed. Doc allowed himself to fall with her onto the sheets. He ran his hands over the smooth contours of her flesh, and his lips wandered over her skin. His tongue darted across her nipples as her soft hand enclosed and squeezed his rock-hard organ.

Charlene slowly slid down along him until the tip of his cock touched the opening of her warm moist sex, which was palpitating in her maddening need for him.

Her fingers lightly held his distended member and was about to guide its great knob into her hungering interior when gunfire—rifles, shotguns, revolvers—broke out all over town.

Doc paused.

"They sure got great timing," he said.

Like any western town, Hugoton paid no great heed to strangers passing through. In fact, Hugoton, being on the Chisholm Trail, had more than a normal flow of new faces, seen an hour, maybe a day, never seen again. It was how strangers behaved, not the mere fact that they were strangers, that drew attention.

When horsemen arriving for the first time in town didn't head right away for one of the saloons, fancy houses, or gaming places and didn't bother with the livery stables or the hotel, that behavior was out of the ordinary. When two came from one direction, three from the opposite way, and then another two from the first direction, all within fifteen minutes of each other, each pair or trio pretending not to know the others, standing about next to their horses tied to hitching rails, seeming in no great hurry and just looking around them, looking every which way except in the direction of the Western National Bank across the street, that was when the town marshal got fast word, unlocked the gun rack in his office, and handed out long guns to whoever was there, freeing a couple of his prisoners and telling them that maybe here was a legal opportunity for them to disturb the peace.

Mad Mike did just that, and the Kid passed out rifles and shotguns to some men who had come in to complain about things other than strangers floating like buzzards about the town bank. The two cowhands from the drunk tank got their guns back and a promise to let bygones be bygones.

In Hogan's Hardware Store, the owner and his clerk passed around guns and ammunition, and the newly armed

townspeople who had been lounging inside—for Hogan was
a good storyteller—now peered out through the dirty window onto the street at the seven strangers loitering opposite
the bank.

One man asked impatiently, "What's holding them up?"

"They're the ones doing the holding up."

"I meant what's delaying them?"

"Danged if I know."

Then they saw the reason and snickered. The bank manager and his clerk came out of the First and Last saloon and
made their way back to their place of business. The manager
fished a large key from his coat pocket and unlocked the
door. It was well known that unscheduled bank closings of
various durations occurred frequently during the day so the
staff could seek refreshment. The robbers had been unlucky.
They had hit town at the wrong time and were left kicking
their heels in the street.

"They must think we're real dumb not to spot this shit,"
Mad Mike muttered to the Kid as he watched from a crack
in the door of the marshal's office, along with his armed
group. "Or else maybe they're the ones who're so dumb
they think no one sees nothing."

The Kid was calmly chewing on a toothpick, with a
strange glitter in his eyes. He didn't say anything.

Two of the strangers stayed with the horses while the
other five walked across the street. One stayed at the bank
door; four went inside. Some wagons and a few horsemen
passed up and down the street. There was a cool evening
breeze as the sun began to set, and if the town didn't look
pretty, it looked quiet and slow-moving.

In less than four minutes the gunmen came out of the
bank. Two carried small grain sacks. They made for their
horses in a hurry.

From the door of his hardware store, Hogan started the

war by shooting one of the men guarding the horses. He hit him in the back from about fifteen yards with a shotgun—he could hardly have missed—and ducked back in his store again.

"Let's go!" Mad Mike yelled to everybody in the marshal's office and burst through the door into the street. Right away, before the others following him could block his view, he dropped to one knee, fired his Winchester .44 rifle, and brought down one of the men carrying the bags.

The Kid was in the lead as the others charged forward. His teeth were bared in a savage grin as he ran as fast as he could, firing from the hip with his Winchester repeater as he went. He tore the left arm off one of the robbers—not clean off the shoulder, but the bullet shattered the part where the upper arm one articulated with the shoulder blade, and left the limb dangling uselessly, held on by only tattered skin and muscle.

The Kid hit his second victim in the upper thigh and stopped him. Then the Kid halted his rush to take careful aim with his rifle and put a bullet in the man's right earhole. The robber's brains were drilled through, and he fell like a dropped broom handle.

Lazy-moving passersby, who moments before the shooting were lounging along like it would take an earthquake to shake them, were diving behind barrels and beneath the timber sidewalk with acrobatic agility. Horses were rearing on their hind legs as high as their reins let them, and a few broke loose from the hitching posts and galloped off down the middle of the street.

The men in Hogan's Hardware Store had a surge of courage after they saw four of the seven bank robbers downed, and they ran headlong out into the street, firing wildly.

The outlaws still on their feet were about to mount their

horses, and they blasted away at these new attackers. One of the men from the hardware store took a slug in his ample gut, and he died on his knees, clutching his belly. Another was hit in the side of the forehead by a bullet from an old Henry .44 rifle, which in spite of its age did a lethal job. A third was hit high in the left shoulder. None of them scored a hit on the bank robbers. Hogan himself had stayed inside his store this time, intending to survive the incident which would make such a good future story.

Only one robber managed to saddle up and ride away. Mad Mike got him when he came back to grab the money sack out of the hands of another who had just been shot. The man tumbled out of the saddle and then lay still in the dust.

One was left standing. He ran and grabbed the sack, then headed for the horses. He didn't have a chance. He ran against the hail of bullets with his head down, like he was facing into a strong wind.

Raider stepped through the batwing doors of the First and Last in time to see him, riddled with bullets, slump mortally wounded in the street.

As he died in the dirt, his grip never loosened on the neck of the grain sack holding the money.

Upon reflection, Myles Lyman decided that his plan to raise funds by robbing the Western National Bank in Hugoton had deserved to fail. The men he had sent on the job were all half-wits. They had to be. Otherwise he couldn't have trusted them to bring the money back to him in Coronado. Anyway, he hadn't trusted them. Turk Calhoun and Snead had been waiting for them in the dusk outside Hugoton in case they took off in some direction other than Coronado.

It was Turk who brought him the news of all the shooting

and no riders breaking loose of the town. Later he heard they had all been killed, which was just as well, since dead men don't tell tales. It served him right, Myles told himself. He hired less than the best and got a botched job in return. That was the trouble. Hired guns came cheap; hired brains were rare at any price.

Calhoun and Snead had brains. They didn't pretend any loyalty or honesty, but then they didn't seem to even care about money. Myles had been right in his guess that Calhoun would lose the money as fast the next day as he had made it on the gaming tables the previous day. He and Snead—or rather, Turk alone decided, and Snead as always did whatever Turk did—took free food, booze, women, and hotel rooms in exchange for "enforcing law and order along with protecting the citizens of Coronado." The town marshal had resigned in protest, and Myles had fixed it for the next town council so Turk would get to wear the star.

In spite of the bank robbery fiasco, things were getting organized for Myles in Coronado. He was coming up against very little resistance from the residents as he began to exert more control over the town. It was as if they had just been waiting for someone to come in and take over. Myles was careful where he stepped, of course, and he went out of his way to hear everyone's opinion and to make it seem that whatever was done was a result of their wishes instead of his own. Myles was amused at his own transformation from confidence trickster to diplomat.

The fact remained that he still hadn't raised cash in quantities sufficient to set himself up as a cattle dealer in competition with Murdock and the others in Hugoton. And he was determined not to touch a penny of his own money. After all, he still had principles. If trying to rob the bank in Hugoton had been a dumb move, it had been the only one open to him, because there was no cash to be raised in

Coronado. All available money was already committed to luring the railroad to the town, and that was something Myles favored as much as everyone else. So if he couldn't raise money to deal in cattle himself at the present time, he could at least try to stop Murdock, Lynch, and Coulter from making their deals.

The dust raised by the traveling herd could be seen from miles away the previous evening. Myles knew they wouldn't get near enough to Hugoton that day and resolved to be out at their camp at dawn. When he arrived, the cook was still yelling at the dog-tired cowhands trying to get a few more minutes sleep in their blankets on the ground around the cooking fire.

The trail boss and two horse wranglers were already drinking coffee and eating steak and beans, adding their own curses and taunts to the cook's shouts at the exhausted cowhands.

The trail boss beckoned to Myles and, pointing to a platter of food and the coffeepot, motioned for him to help himself. "If they were outside some dang saloon or whorehouse, you think these varmints would be feeling so stiff and wore out?"

"You boys have a rough time?" Myles inquired sympathetically as he helped himsef to steak and beans.

"Wildest damn longhorns in Texas," the trail boss said, his mouth full. "We took them off three ranches over on the Pecos. These goddamn beasts have ranged where they pleased all their lives, and they ain't changing now. We got 'em tired out by keeping them on the hoof most of the time, but for a long while it looked like they might get us wore out first. You a gambler, mister?"

"No," Lyman said. "I'm a businessman."

The trail boss grinned. He had been amused to meet this gray-haired dude in his fancy gaming room outfit at daybreak on the plains. He figured he must be in some kind of trouble to be riding out at such an hour.

Myles said, "I should warn you boys to stay clear of Hugoton."

"Why?" the trail boss asked. "I was thinking of maybe selling off this herd there, if they give me a good offer, instead of spending another week taking it up to Wichita. I'll be glad to see the end of these critters."

"A word to the wise," Lyman said. "Take your herd where you'll get good money. You'll be done dirty in Hugoton, I tell you that. If you need supplies, stop off in Coronado. That's a good town. Know what they call Hugoton around here? Scumville."

Myles talked on with them until the cowboys had eaten and the herd was about to be moved. After Myles had gone, some of the men approached the trail boss.

"You going to listen to that old buzzard, Luke? You going to pass by Hugoton?"

The trail boss laughed. "I liked that old trickster's style. But you know me. If I hadn't been going to look in on Hugoton before I met him, I sure as hell am now. And I'll get rid of these dang cows there too if I get the right price. You think I'd believe that sharp character in his gambler's clothes, who never worked a day in his life, out on the range at daybreak? All right, men, move them on out!"

Charlene was woken by a knock on the door. She had been lying on the bed fully clothed, taking a nap. The knock sounded again.

"Who is it?"

"Let me in."

"Is that you, Doc? No, it isn't. Who are you?"

"Open up."

She peered through the window. It was Jim Coulter. "Go away."

"I want to talk with you, Charlene. It's Jim."

"I don't want to talk with you, Mr. Coulter. Now go away."

"Let me in, Charlene."

"Not on your life."

He kicked the door, then threw his shoulder against it. But the door was constructed of heavy pine planks with stout crosspieces and a big iron lock. Coulter saw that this door would break him down before he it. He heard Charlene on the inside slide across another bolt. Just like a woman, he thought. She barricades the door and feels safe—while nothing but a sheet of thin glass protects her in the window.

Coulter took off his suit coat, draped it over his head and right shoulder, and dived through the window. The glass shattered, and he ended up on the carpet with a few minor cuts. He looked up, very pleased with himself, at Charlene—and was surprised to discover he was looking into the barrels of a miniature over-and-under. Charlene was holding the little two-shot Remington .41 in a trembling hand, sobbing with rage.

"Take it easy, little angel, take it real gentle," Jim Coulter said in what he hoped was a calming voice. He was genuinely alarmed that she might discharge the weapon in her disturbed state.

"You just climb back out that window, you bastard!"

"Now, Charlene, you don't really mean that."

"I sure do." She touched his forehead with the little pistol's muzzles. "If you don't start to move out of here, I'll kill you."

He moved all right. There was no way he could draw his six-gun without her noticing, so he simply jerked his head to one side, out of the path of the over-and-under barrels, and swatted the pistol out of her hand. It hit the carpet and did not discharge.

Coulter gripped her wrist and yanked her down on the glass-sprinkled carpet beside him. He leered at her. "Now we got a chance at last to have a nice talk."

She hit him in the face with her fist. Then she had to squeeze her fingers because she had hurt her hand hitting him and not hurt him at all. He laughed at her and licked his thick coarse lips in his red face.

"I'm going to make it so you're going to enjoy a real man, doll, instead of that slick quack you been hanging out with. Let me see them knockers of yours."

He caught his fingers in the neck of her dress and ripped a strip of the silk material from the front of her body.

Charlene looked down in surprised outrage at her suddenly bared body, then raked her nails down Jim Coulter's face.

He grunted with pain, cursed, and slugged her with his fist. She slumped back, dazed, until he began to tug her clothes down over her hips. She screamed and threshed around, yelled for help and scratched, pulled his hair and hammered on him with her fists.

Doc Weatherbee, on his way to see Charlene, heard her screams while still up the street a ways and noticed the shattered window. He broke into a run and dove clean through the window.

The Pinkerton landed with a lot of force on Coulter's back as the cattleman was ripping away the final remnants of Charlene's clothes. The two men tumbled across the room, carried by the force of Weatherbee's dive. Doc climbed to one knee and drove his fist into Coulter's face. The cattleman rolled away out of his reach. Jim Coulter knew better now than to trade punches with the Pinkerton. Still lying on the floor, he drew his revolver and squeezed off a fast shot at Doc before the Pinkerton could get out of its way.

Doc felt the agonizing sear of the bullet ripping through his flesh. He fought against the pain in his right side, trying to focus on Coulter and where the next bullet would be coming from. But the violent twisting hurt was too much for him and overcame his ability to see and think clearly. Doc could think only of one thing to do. He threw himself behind a heavy oak chest, and the second bullet missed him and buried itself in the wall.

All Coulter had to do was to get up off the floor so he could get a shot at Doc behind the chest. As he scrambled to his feet, he paid no attention to Charlene. Clutching a piece of her ripped dress to her front, she groped for the .41 Remington over-and-under that he had knocked from her hand earlier. She picked up the derringer-sized pistol and fired a shot at Coulter before he could squeeze the trigger at Doc for the third time.

Jim Coulter took the big .41 slug from the miniature pistol in the side of his face. The hurtling lump of lead crushed his cheekbone and sheared through his skull like a spoon opening an egg. The projectile exited through the top of his head, leaving it split open and leaking its contents.

Raider left Weatherbee at the doctor's dispensary, where he was having the livid furrow cut by Jim Coulter's bullet cleaned and bandaged. The bullet had hit his ribs at an angle and bounced off instead of penetrating. Doc had been lucky. When Doc asked after Charlene, Raider told him she was all right and resting. He lied.

After he left the dispensary, Raider stopped off at his room in the Eagle Hotel to collect his .30-.30 Winchester carbine and then continued on to the marshal's office. Mad

Mike and the Kid were waiting for him. He had expected that.

Raider sat in a chair facing them and then stood again, making it plain he was doing so to handle his carbine more readily, should he be needed to do so.

"You see Tom Murdock or Rob Lynch around?" Raider asked.

"I expect they're in the First and Last, mourning the loss of their friend," Mad Mike said.

The Kid was looking from one to the other, waiting for the shooting to get started.

Raider went to the doorway and tossed a quarter to a passing boy. "Tell Mr. Murdock and Mr. Lynch they're needed bad at the marshal's office."

"They pay me as a marshal of this town," Mad Mike called from behind him. "You got any talk about getting that murdering bitch outa jail, you talk with me."

Raider ignored him and strolled back inside to resume the standoff between him and the Kid.

In a little while a voice called from the street, "What's going on in there?"

"Come on in, Mr. Murdock," Raider called back. "You too, Mr. Lynch."

"Ain't no need for you to come in," Mad Mike shouted. "Me and the Kid have this situation under control. You may take your leave, gentlemen, and rest assured all is well."

"You ain't taking no leave after you put an innocent woman in jail for saving her own and my partner's lives. You drag her out of her home, hardly letting her get clothes on, and throw her in a cell for killing a no-good coyote who if he had survived would be charged with attempted murder and rape. It so happens this coyote was a pal of yours. Now that ain't no reason in my eyes why she should go to jail after saving my partner's life. And I want you two excellent gentlemen to know I'm holding a carbine in my hands and if you try to walk away from here without telling your boys to release that woman, sure as God I'll blast you in your tracks soon as you start to move away."

"That's all right, Mr. Murdock," Mad Mike called. "He has to turn his back on us to shoot you and Mr. Lynch."

"If I have to shoot your two lackeys here in order to have a shot at you, Murdock," Raider ground out, "you can be sure as hell I ain't sparing your hide."

Murdock called, "Mike, can we talk with you here?"

Mad Mike turned to the Kid. "Watch him but don't start nothing."

The Kid nodded sullenly and Mad Mike went out the door of the marshal's office into the street.

Raider looked the Kid hard in the face. The Kid eyed Raider in open hate.

"You real fast, Kid?" Raider asked with a grin and moved threateningly closer, holding his carbine sideways in front of his body.

"I kin draw faster'n you can twist that carbine barrel on me," the Kid said confidently.

Raider spat in his face.

The Kid went for his gun. Raider whipped around the wood stock of the carbine and caught the Kid across the side of the head with the butt end of the shoulder rest. The wood made a solid thump, and the Kid dropped like a moth hit with a rolled newspaper.

The keys to the cells were in the desk drawer. Raider opened the door at the back of the office and released Charlene from her cell.

"Doc is okay," he assured her. "Now go straight home."

Mad Mike, Murdock, and Lynch were still arguing in the middle of the street when they saw Charlene emerge from the doorway of the marshal's office and head down the street toward her cabin. Her walk was graceful and unhurried—that of a beautiful woman who knows all eyes are on her.

The three men looked from her to the marshal's office and back again. Everything was very quiet.

Rob Lynch said to the others, "I got the feeling someone's looking along the sights of a carbine at us this very moment. How about I buy you both a drink at the First and Last?"

Mike and Murdock followed him there.

CHAPTER NINE

Myles Lyman felt good about leaving Coronado in the hands of its new marshal and deputy marshal, Turk Calhoun and Snead. They were born drifters. He would use them for whatever they were worth while he had the chance to do so and discard them when they had served their purpose or replace them if they moved on, whichever came first. Most important, they were not competition to him, since they wanted no stake in Coronado.

Myles was very pleased to hear of the death of Jim Coulter, whom he regarded as the most dangerous of the three cattlemen that controlled Hugoton. Now that Coulter and Seattle Bill were gone, things were really looking up for Coronado. If it came to gunslinging, Coronado could pretty much hold its own, he figured.

In the meantime he was not wasting a day. There were times when he even forgot altogether for a few hours about the two Pinkertons just lying there in wait for him. He'd

show those two interfering bastards who was smarter. He'd
send them back to that Scottish troublemaker in Chicago
with their tails between their legs. After that, every time
Allan Pinkerton heard the name Myles Lyman he would
wince and change the subject of conversation.

But it wasn't in Lyman's nature to sit back and let events
work themselves out. An idea had occurred to him while
reading a newspaper a few days before. The journalist who
penned the long article that cuaght his interest bewailed the
frequent destruction of towns by fire. Whole communities
were wiped out in a matter of hours, usually without many
casualties and often without any. This was nothing new to
Myles. What caught his attention was the remark that Kansas
towns that burned to the ground often never got rebuilt if
they weren't on a railroad line because of the lack of timber
in the state and the difficulties of transporting quantities of
lumber overland without a railroad. Existing towns had grown
bit by bit, not overnight. Burned-out, homeless townspeople
were often more likely to move elsewhere, the article stated,
than stick around to wait on supplies in order to rebuild.
The consequences of such a tragedy striking Hugoton brought
a warm smile to his tired face.

What he needed were outsiders—people no one could
connect with Coronado—to ride into Hugoton and torch
the place. What he also needed was to keep his mouth shut,
to keep the idea to himself, because if people got burned
alive and he was blamed for it, real fast he'd find himself
dancing on the end of a rope. Folks tended to take badly
to town-burners.

This morning Myles was riding out to a work camp he
had heard about where men were making adobe bricks.
Myles could not imagine who was going to buy these bricks
or what they could be used for out here on the plains—
until he reached the area and saw that farmers had plowed

up the grassland. He hadn't heard that farmers had pushed this far west in Kansas. Since his own plans for the future now involved cattle, he had taken a sudden dislike to these nesters and their barbed wire who cut off tracts of the plains—free and open to all—for their private use.

Myles came to the brickworks because he figured that anyone digging mud for a living would be pleased to get the offer of a job as a firebrand for triple what he was presently earning. True, those involved might have to rapidly cross the line into the Indian Territory to escape the law, but Myles figured that a man reduced to digging mud for a living could have no great fondness for or attachment to Kansas anyway.

He watched them dig the soil and mix it with water until it was a thick mud. Then they added straw from that summer's wheat crop. The men pressed the mud-and-straw mixture into wooden molds more than a foot long, more than half a foot wide, and a few inches deep. In another area he could see how the dried-out bricks shrank inside the molds. Men had only to turn the wooden molds upside down for the bricks to fall out. They placed these bricks on the ground to harden further in the sun.

"You looking for a job maybe?" a hearty farmer type said by way of a greeting.

"I think not," Myles said condescendingly.

"You may not think much of what you see here at this moment, mister, but when we get things properly set up in time, you'll ride into this place and you won't realize you ever set eyes on it before."

Myles saw the truth in what the man was saying. "You mean you'll have tree-lined streets and schools and a bank and so forth."

"First we have to build grain-storage buildings and better houses for ourselves. Over yonder rise in the ground, you'll see where we live now—in sod houses. We'll build decent dry dwelling places for ourselves with these bricks and have places to store our grain and other food supplies so we can survive drought years."

In spite of himself, Myles found himself interested in their enterprise. He toured the settlement with his guide and made constructive comments where he could. He knew he was wasting his time here, that these dedicated nesters would be horrified at an offer from him to make quick money at arson. Yet he stayed on and even accepted an invitation to the town dance that was to be held that evening in the community hall, one of three timber buildings in this little settlement of huts with sod walls and grass growing on their roofs. All three timber buildings had had wheels attached and had been towed there from other towns. Of the other two, one was a church and the other a school—a big one-room cabin that still bore foot-high red letters on its front: SALOON. The pupils sat on empty beer kegs before the bar, which served the teacher as her desk. There was no place in town a man could buy a drink, and they were proud of the fact that this was a dry community. Over the years, Myles Lyman had forgotten that places like this existed.

Strong coal-black coffee was the most potent drink to be had at the dance. Thick ham and deviled egg sandwiches were followed by big slices of homemade chocolate cake and cream cakes. The schoolchildren recited some patriotic verses while the fiddlers put resin on their bows. Then the dancing began. And continued late into the night. Babies and young children slept everywhere, huddled in blankets.

Myles Lyman slept under the open sky, wrapped in a borrowed blanket. He saw the eastern horizon slowly gray with the approaching morning and thought things over. He was getting on in life. Was it too late for him to make a fresh start? He was too old now to undertake the hard labor of tilling the soil, but he had more than enough money set aside to hire others to do the work. He had danced a great deal of the time with an attractive widow a little younger than himself.

Before Myles Lyman closed his eyes, he had made up his mind to cease his evil ways, come to this settlement, and revive the pioneering spirit he had so strongly possessed as a young man, before he went wrong.

As his pleasantly tired body and newly tranquil mind slowly sank into sleep, Myles felt happy for the first time in years.

The stage from Wichita arrived along the dusty rutted main street of Hugoton and pulled up in front of the livery stables.

"No passengers descending at Hugoton today," the driver shouted to the stablemen. "I have some barrels and chests to unload, that's all. Give me some good horses this time, hear? Those were all cripples you harnessed to the stage last time."

As the driver and stablemen exchanged good-natured abuse, the passengers climbed out of the stage, some to stretch their legs, others to hurry off to the nearest saloon. But before any of them got anywhere, two men ran out of the First and Last saloon, one chasing the other through the batwing doors. The man behind drew his revolver and fired two shots at the fleeing man, who staggered and fell face down in the middle of the street. His hat rolled away in the dust.

The gunman holstered his smoking revolver and turned back toward the saloon doors, strolling casually away from the still body lying in the dirt. The gunman was big and broad-shouldered. He wore a scarred black leather jacket, faded denims, and a black Stetson. What struck the stage passengers particularly were his jet-black eyes and his big mustache.

The town marshal and a man with a deputy's badge confronted the gunman at the batwing doors to the saloon. Their guns were drawn—they had the drop on the big killer.

"Raider," the marshal said, "you're a no-good horse thief, and in these parts that's about as bad as a man can do. Kid, go fetch a length of rope. It's time we seen justice done. There'll be no horse stealing hereabouts while I'm marshal of this town."

"To hell with you and justice, Mad Mike," Raider spat in contempt.

While two men dragged away the corpse from the street, Mad Mike and the Kid walked Raider at gunpoint to a porch down the street, over which the Kid tossed the rope and tied a noose.

One of the stage passengers said with indignation to the others, "That marshal cares nothing for the man we saw killed. All he cares about is horse stealing."

"I have no objection to hanging horse thieves," another said, "but I think it fair he gets a trial. Not to mention what you said about rustling horses being a more serious crime than murder in this town. I'm getting right back in this stage this very moment and won't relax again till I'm out of this horrible primitive place."

But they had to wait because their driver was going nowhere, be told them, till he had seen the hanging. "This town's so bad," he went on to say, "that last year I had this fine eastern lady come here to review the educational system in this here town. Anyways, just as she was stepping down off the stage, there happened to be three or four fights going on—you know, they were spilling out of saloons into the streets and punching each other and firing their Colts. Of course they were all so lit they could hit hardly nothing, and only a few were killed. But this fine lady, she steps right back into the stage and demands that we leave town immediately. I says to her—but hold it, they're ready now to string him up. Watch this, they don't let him drop off a horse or a chair in this town. They haul him up from his feet so he strangles slowly instead of dying from a snapped neckbone. Twice as painful, so they say. Watch now—there he goes!"

They saw the man dragged off the ground at the end of the rope and dangle, with his legs kicking, beneath the porch.

"These people are savages," one passenger remarked, and the others agreed. They climbed inside the coach. "We are ready when you are, sir," one called to the driver.

"Right ho, then, we'll be off." The driver winked at the stablemen and cracked his whip over the fresh horses.

After the stage had trundled out of town, laughing townspeople lowered Raider to the ground. He took the rope from beneath his armpits, where it had been instead of around his neck, and accepted a dozen separate offers of a drink. It had been the best stunt in town all day. The "corpse" was brushing dust off his shirt.

Mad Mike was saying, "Dang it, them passengers will be telling this story to the end of their days, about how they rode into the wild town of Hugoton and saw an hombre strung up for stealing a horse and not blamed for shooting a man in the back. I got to give it to you, Raider, it went perfect."

Only Doc Weatherbee was not amused. His wound was healing nicely but was still giving him a lot of pain. He was irritable.

"Raider, do you think that crude jokes like this are worthy of a Pinkerton operative?" he asked in a judgmental tone.

"Better than being creased by a bullet in the ribs in a

room with a naked woman," Raider replied.

Doc laughed, which made his ribs hurt all the more.

When Myles Lyman woke beneath his blanket on the hard ground at the farming community, he sat up and looked about him. He remembered his vow of the night before—that he would come and settle with these fine people, giving up a life of underhanded schemes to return to the simple basics of pioneer values—and he wondered what could possibly have made him feel that way about this godforsaken place where men had to toil like beasts simply to survive.

He looked around the settlement again, barely nodding to the cheerful greetings he received on the way. The noise of the children irritated him. Everyone's optimism and friendliness were too much of a good thing—he wasn't in the mood for it today. If these idiots preferred to wallow in mud rather than pick up some easy cash by burning down Hugoton for him, they were welcome to it. He was getting out of here.

Besides, an idea had occurred to him from a conversation the previous evening. Most of his talks with the farmers seemed to have centered around natural phenomena. Droughts were a big subject. So were grasshoppers. The grasshoppers, when they came, hit in swarms that filled every inch of sky and devoured every blade of grass and sprout of wheat. The insect hordes were like a plague out of the Bible, and naturally the God-fearing farmers often wondered if their own misdeeds had brought this scourge upon themselves as a sign from above. Especially when farmers in one area would be hard hit and some elsewhere would have crops untouched.

The farmers in this settlement had a fallback arranged if drought or 'hoppers cleaned them out. They could pick bones.

"When the Union Pacific hired Buffalo Bill Cody to provide meat for their railroadmen back in 1871 or so, he killed more than four thousand buffalo in a year and a half," one farmer told Myles. "That ain't even counting all them other buffalo hunters who was just looking for their skins and left their meat to rot where they shot them. And them they call sportsmen—some of them come all the way from Europe—princes, dukes, and the like, just to blast away at the huge herds of them big dumb animals."

"I once saw a professional hunter kill a hundred and twenty in forty minutes," another man said. "Saw it with my own eyes."

"I believe you," the first farmer continued. "A few years ago you could travel for days and stay in sight of one huge herd. Some of them professional hunters made a hundred dollars a day when the going was good, back when the herds was more plentiful than swarms of flies is today."

"Yeah, and they used to kill 'em like flies too."

"First time my wife saw bleached buffalo bones stretched across the prairie far as the horizon, she said, 'Look, John, all the lilies.' She was mighty upset when them lilies in the distance turned out to be sun-dried bones close up."

"Yet you was mightly glad, after your crops failed, to haul cartloads of them bones to the railhead so they could be shipped to the fertilizer factory."

That had been it. The men Myles needed for the job on Hugoton. Men down on their luck. Bone pickers. They'd do it and be glad of the work.

"Bone pickers!" a man snorted in disgust to Doc Weatherbee, as two large wagons and six horsemen made their way along the main street of Hugoton. "Times must be hard if they're foraging this far from a railhead."

The six horsemen and two wagon drivers looked beaten and half starved. They stared around them with almost glazed eyes, not responsive, strongly fearful.

"Sorry-looking sight they make," the man continued scornfully to Doc. "They'll buy some salted pork in town maybe, and beans and some bottles of cheap rotgut, sleep under those wagons at the edge of town tonight, and push on tomorrow. A lot of the bone pickers are farmers wiped out by a drought or grasshoppers, but not this crew. These men probably came out west 'cause they thought life would be easy. Well, they found what they came for with these buffalo bones—easy picking!" He laughed at his own joke.

It was much later that Weatherbee recalled the bone pickers' arrival in town and this man's remarks about them. Doc hadn't noticed them again during the day. If they had spent their time in town, it hadn't been at the Eagle Hotel or at the First and Last. Doc supposed that if they had occupied their time in a saloon, it would have been at one of the little places with a canvas roof and with a couple of boards stretched between two crates for a bar over the dirt floor.

The cry "Fire!" sounded well after midnight. It was picked up along the street. A porter hammered the gong in the lobby of the Eagle Hotel and yelled at the top of his voice, "Fire! Fire! Man says this town's afire!"

Raider tumbled out of bed where he had been asleep in his clothes. He had already buckled on his six-gun and stepped into his boots before he shook himself fully awake. He grabbed his Stetson off the chest of drawers and headed out the door for the stairs.

Doc and Charlene dressed quickly and filled buckets with water to protect her cabin. This was no selfish action. It was up to the owner of each building to protect his or her own property, and if the building owner was successful in

saving his own place, he did everyone else a favor by stopping the fire spreading in that direction. They could see no
alarming glow from outside her window, and when Doc
went outside, he saw three small fires against the sides of
buildings. These were all well under control as men threw
water or dry dirt on them.

A cabin on the opposite side of the street from Charlene's
home suddenly began to blaze. Apparently no one had seen
the flames at the rear of the cabin, and now tongues of fire
were already lapping the whole back wall and eaves of the
roof. Doc helped others get an elderly storekeeper in a
nightshirt and his wailing wife in a shift out of the burning
cabin. They tried to put the flames out, but it was too late.
The fire had truly caught hold. So Doc and the others rescued
as many of the old couple's possessions as they could.

The storekeeper grabbed Doc by the arm as he was about
to run back into the smoky interior for another chair. "Listen
to me, Doc. I know you're a Pinkerton, and that makes you
an honest man. Our life savings are in there—everything
my wife and I have put aside over the years. There's a small
flat wooden box beneath a loose floorboard—the fifth back
from the front wall to the left of the doorway. Get it for us,
Doc, for God's sake. It's all we've got for our old age."

Doc nodded and darted inside the door of the burning
cabin. By this time the other men had given up recovering
the couple's possessions because the smoke had grown too
dense and it was impossible either to see or breathe inside.

Weatherbee turned left inside the door, holding his breath,
his eyes already irritated and tearing from the pungent smoke.
He flattened his face against the wall and breathed the inch
of pure air sandwiched between the smoke and solid material. He tore with his fingers at a board that he couldn't
budge. After he had wiped the tears from his eyes and filled

his lungs with more or less breathable air from the thin layer next to the wall, he stopped again and tried the board next to the one he had tried before. The board was loose. The lumber board was heavy and loose-fitting, adzed rather than sawed, so he had no difficulty in getting his fingers into the crack between that board and the next and lifting up.

Doc could see nothing underneath. He lifted up the whole length of board, set it on the floor, and felt with his hands in the dirt beneath the floorboards. Nothing. He had to stand to expel the air from his lungs and take another deep breath. This time the thin layer next to the wall had become so tainted he coughed violently. Then he dropped to his knees and felt with his hands on the crumbly soil in the darkness beneath the floorboards.

His fingers touched a corner of the box, and it shifted a little as his hand brushed against it. He used both hands to lift the box out. It was many times heavier than its small size would normally suggest. Gold, Doc knew. He put the box under his arm and ran for the door, now only a pale rectangle through the black and gray coiling smoke.

It was only after he got back to Charlene's and happened to catch a look at himself in her full-length mirror that Doc paled in horror.

His face and silk shirt were grimy from the smoke, and some burned wood had left a huge black streak down the side of his best jacket.

Raider passed buckets of water in a line to a burning store near the Eagle Hotel. He and the others managed to quench the flames before they consumed the building. After that he and the others patrolled the town, lending a hand where they could and watching for airborne sparks or embers that might land on roofs and start fresh fires.

He was still looking around him when Mad Mike, the Kid, and some others passed on their way to the stables.

"We found out who done it, Raider," Mad Mike shouted. "Come along with us to the stable, saddle up, and we'll go after them."

A young boy had woken and gone outside to the rear of his family's cabin to take a leak. He had seen men run by the cabins on each side of the street throwing bundles of something against every third building. Then others came along behind them holding lengths of wood with flaming oil-soaked rags at their tips. They touched the bundles against the cabins with their torches and the fires started. The boy stood where he was in the shadows till they had gone. Then he ran inside, roused his father, and this man raised the alarm with cries of fire.

"We found scorched bundles of dried prairie grass at some of the quenched fires," Mike said. "I've just been holding some of them. Smell this."

Raider smelled Mike's hands. Kerosene.

"And the boy saw who done it, too," Mike added as they neared the stables. "Them bone pickers who rode into town today."

Raider saddled up along with the others in the livery stables. Although he and Mad Mike and the Kid had learned to exist with each other—mostly by taking care to keep away from each other, except for occasional pranks such as the fake murder and hanging—Raider would never have foreseen himself riding by their side as part of a town posse after wrongdoers. But he had seen badmen wearing a marshal's badge before—and even sometimes, out of pure orneriness and cussedness, make a good job of it. So he rode along, expecting Weatherbee to appear at any moment to inform him it was against Pinkerton regulations.

"They were camped by the side of the trail out this way just before sundown," the townsman leading them called back.

"I expect they'll have moved by now," Mad Mike said. "We'll circle about and lay eyes on 'em at first light."

The horses kept to the trail in the darkness, seeming to find no difficulty in navigating by starlight. The men let them set their own pace and grew silent, peering ahead into the night as they thought they were nearing the place where the bone pickers had last been seen.

They were still there. One of the men lit an oil lamp, and they all drew their guns.

"What do you folks want this hour of the night?" one of the bone pickers called from beneath a wagon.

An oil lamp flared on the ground, and they could see the men lying there covered with their blankets.

"They've had time to get back here and pretend to have slept through everything," the Kid rasped to Mad Mike.

"Maybe," Mike replied.

They dismounted and looked around with the help of more lamps. The campfire had been dead some time. The horses were tied on long halters to one of the wagons. It certainly looked like no one had been away from this camp after nightfall. The Kid was searching the wagons.

"Smell their hands, Raider," Mike said grimly.

Kerosene.

"Smell this!" the Kid yelled from one wagon, holding up a ten-gallon earthen crock.

He poured its contents over the nearest bone picker on the ground beneath him. Before Raider could stop him, the Kid struck a match and tossed it on the freshly doused bone picker, who was trying to wipe the stinging liquid out of his eyes.

The man's body lit up in small dancing flames all over. He screamed and ran in circles about the place, waving his arms, his flame-flickered figure in the darkness looking more like something out of a fiesta display than a real human in the throes of an agonized death.

Raider grabbed one of the blankets from beneath the wagon and chased after the man. He succeeded in wrapping the blanket around him from head to toe, and then he rolled him on the ground till he made sure all the flames were extinguished.

When Raider unwrapped the blanket, his stomach heaved at the smell of singed flesh and the sight of the blackened body. He knew the man was still alive only because of his moans and the spasmodic jerks of his carbonized limbs.

One of the bone pickers drew a revolver. He walked up to stand above his burned companion, pointed the gun, and put a bullet in his brain. The bone picker tossed his revolver on the ground—much to the Kid's amazement, since he was ready and waiting for the bone picker to turn on him.

While they were tying their seven prisoners' hands behind their backs and getting set to put them in one of the wagons to take them back to town, the Kid searched the corpse's charred denims. He whooped and held up a mint-fresh twenty-dollar gold piece in the lamplight. Then he ran from man to man of the bone pickers and found on each a single twenty-dollar gold piece.

"I'm rich! Rich!" the Kid howled. "Shit, we're going to drink up every penny of this in the First and Last. We'll have ourselves a hanging party and celebrate till it gets daylight enough to string these seven coyotes all in a row."

"Each had a twenty-dollar gold piece," Doc said ruminatively over a glass of the First and Last's best bourbon, which was flowing freely for all present at the Kid's hanging party. "So someone was paying them to burn down Hugoton. Lyman would never be dumb enough to try anything like that. Or would he? But he'd cover his tracks so these hired goons wouldn't know him by name. Still and all . . ."

Raider nodded. "It's worth a try."

"Better bring Mad Mike with us while he's still fairly sober."

They had to bring a bottle of bourbon with them before Mike was willing to leave the saloon. "All right," he agreed. "I'll keep my mouth shut no matter what you say. Only thing is, they ain't none of them leaving that cell for one second, and don't try nothing when my back is turned or try to feed me poison from this bottle, thinking it's going to addle my brains. My brains got addled a long time ago. Bourbon ain't going to change my mind about nothing."

"Sit and listen," Doc suggested politely.

The seven bone pickers were talking urgently together in one large cell when they went through the rear door of the marshal's office. The men stopped talking.

"Good morning, gentlemen," Doc greeted them. "Please excuse my appearance. We've had an unfortunate happening in town tonight—I believe you're aware of the details— and I haven't had a chance to bathe and change yet. In fact, we've just taken a few minutes off from the hanging party the town is holding right now." Doc held up his glass of bourbon in a toast. "To your necks, gentlemen."

Mad Mike seconded the toast. "I'll drink to that."

Doc resumed. "But we haven't come down here to torment you before your time arrives. I understand that will be at daybreak." Doc was now walking up and down before the barred door of the cell, and the seven men inside were following him back and forth with their eyes like a nestful of mice watching a playful cat. "We came to hear something. I and my friend"—he pointed to Raider—"want to know something badly. If you happen to say what we want to know, you'll go free. Understand that? You won't hang. We brought the marshal along with us so you can believe what we say. Unfortunately, we can't tell you what we want to hear. It's up to you to tell us, and you don't have much time." Doc stopped pacing and faced the seven. "Start talking."

One man did. He was smaller, hungrier-looking, and even more frightened than the others. Not only did the others not try to stop him from talking, they all seemed eager to give their versions of the story so it could be seen they were cooperating too.

"What did you do when this gray-haired dude in a gambler's getup gave you twenty dollars apiece and said there was another twenty each after you had fired this town?" Doc asked after he had heard some of the story.

"First, we decided to take off with the money and do nothing," the bone picker said. "Then we got to worrying maybe he'd send some guns after us. We decided not to take a chance on that. But neither were we going to take a chance on not getting paid the other twenty each if we did . . . eh, the job for him. He didn't give us no name, but he told us we'd find him in the Plain Hell saloon in Coronado after we'd destroyed Hugoton. So we went there first and waited around till we spotted him. He was mad as hell, but we explained things to him and quieted him down. He said no more than three of us was to come next time to collect the money because we was too noticeable. Before we left Coronado, we learned his name was Myles Lyman."

Doc asked, "Would you be willing to be a witness against him in a court of law?"

There was a chorus of yeses.

"Seems like we have something at last on Mr. Lyman," Doc said, "if we can get the marshal to go along with it."

"I ain't letting none of these bastards out of that cell," Mad Mike said firmly. "I said that before I came here, and now I'm saying it again."

"You're beginning to sound like the Kid," Doc observed acidly. "These men are hired fools. They don't count. If you had given them the money, they'd have burned Coronado for you—or tried to, more likely. What satisfaction is there in getting back at them? It's Myles Lyman you want, not them."

Mad Mike sighed, pulled a key from his pocket, and opened the cell door. "You, you, and you. I'll take you to the stables to get your horses. If you three don't get back here with Lyman by high noon, these four hang. I'll put the nooses round their necks myself."

Myles Lyman climbed onto the flat roof of the three-story building that contained the Plain Hell saloon on its first floor. Sure enough he could see a column of smoke rising on the far side of the low hills in the direction of Hugoton.

"How do I know that ain't just prairie grass burning?" he asked the three bone pickers who had climbed up with him.

"'Cause if we set fire to grass, hoping to fool you, it would be burning all along a broad front instead of in one place. And you know how grass smoke looks. That ain't grass smoke. That's wood smoke."

Myles wasn't sure he knew the difference, but he wasn't going to show off his ignorance to bone pickers.

"Well, I reckon I owe you boys your pay, then." He handed over eight twenty-dollar gold pieces. "They never caught up with you?"

"We camped right on the edge of town. We slept through the whole thing. Ain't that right?"

"They believed us. Only thing is they took our two wagons. Paid us. But we didn't want to sell. But they took 'em anyway on account of folks moving away."

Myles grinned. "They're moving away already?"

"Nothing much left to keep them there. 'Cept one small bunch who swears they're going to stay put 'cause of some railroad or something they expect. Well, I reckon we oughta push off back there. Our five buddies is waiting on us."

"In Hugoton?"

"Sure."

"Wait. Let me collect some men and I'll go with you."

While they waited, the bone pickers talked among themselves.

"We're making good time."

"Shit, I thought it was all up when he said it was only grass that was burning. He was righter than he knew. Though I guess them Hugoton boys musta thrown on a few wood planks to make it look good as it does."

"What do we do when we hit the top of them hills and Lyman and the others sees Hugoton ain't burnt to the ground."

"Ride like hell and keep our heads low, unless maybe there's a surprise waiting for 'em in the hills."

"Hush now, here's Lyman coming back with his boys."

"Snead, hold back," Turk Calhoun called softly. "You too, Lyman."

They respectfully did his bidding and let the others ride on ahead of them into the hills. Myles was impatient to get his first glimpse at the burned-over sight of Hugoton from the crest of the hills, but he knew enough to pay heed to the Southerner when the latter spoke in a tone of command.

"Just an old solider being wary," Calhoun explained. He touched the side of his nose. "Maybe all this don't scent real good to an old hound dog like me. Hang back a spell."

The shooting started a few minutes later, and Coronado men began dropping from their saddles.

Lyman, Calhoun, and Snead wheeled their horses around and cantered hell for leather back the way they had come.

CHAPTER TEN

No matter what Weatherbee said about making progress because they now had something definite on Myles Lyman, and had even persuaded a judge to put out an arrest warrant on him for conspiracy to commit arson, Raider felt bored and depressed. He had sent a personal telegram to Chicago to request a transfer, claiming that Weatherbee could handle this case alone, only to find out that Doc had done the same thing himself the previous day, claiming that Raider could manage alone and that the presence of two men was a waste of manpower. They had both received short terse telegrams in reply from Wagner, almost identically worded, telling them to stay put till they apprehended Lyman.

Raider was feeling morose and his gut was troubling him. He blamed it all on his being stuck in a small cowtown with Weatherbee and some others who if he never laid eyes on them again, he wouldn't exactly be broke up. He'd tried riding out of town for hours at a time, but there was nothing much out there except Coronado, and when he'd ridden past there, no one had come out to challenge him. He hadn't ridden close enough to the town to come in range of a rifle. No doubt that's what they were hoping for. Raider just wanted Lyman to know that now he was a wanted man, that there were men hunting for him. He figured Lyman wasn't the sort to lie low and hide in the tall grass—pretty soon he'd make a mad dash for it, escape or attack, it could be either. If Raider was going to be stuck here waiting for him to make his move, he was going to smoke him out somehow real soon.

Other times the big Pinkerton paced uneasily up and down the main street of Hugoton like a caged panther. He even dropped into the stables a few times with carrots or other vegetables—expensive in these parts—for Doc's mule. Not that Judith and he got along any better than usual. He was convinced that once the beast tried to snap off his fingers as he was feeding her. It was just something to do. One local had told him the thing about a small town was that you got to meet all your friends every day, and also all your enemies.

As he walked along the main street, moodily kicking up dirt with the toes of his boots, Raider once again recalled his rage and frustration at seeing Lyman and two others hold back and keep free of the ambush set for them in the range of hills. There was no way he and Doc could have prevented the excited Hugoton men from firing on their Coronado enemies, and Raider could recall perfectly in his mind's eye the galling sight of Lyman's escape on his horse back to Coronado. Later Doc and he had escorted the seven bone pickers clear of the town. They had their forty dollars arson money each, and he and Doc knew where to find them so they could bear witness in court should Lyman be taken alive. Doc would insist on a trial, of course. So far as Raider was concerned, that bastard Lyman would have to be mighty careful if he wanted to live to see the inside of a courtroom.

Raider had slipped into the ways and rhythms of life in the small town more than he realized. Like almost everyone else, he never missed the arrival of the stage. It hit town four times a week, twice traveling west and twice east. When the stage was early, women panicked to fix their hair and change their dresses in time to see the passengers and be seen by them. When the stage was overdue, people walked up and down, and the men talked of the possibility of a broken axle or robbery by road agents while the women whispered about rape by Comanches.

Today the stage was on time, drawn by four steaming horses, filled with passengers and loaded down with baggage. The driver pulled up outside the livery stables. When the stage door opened, everyone stared curiously.

Orville Huggins stepped down onto the dusty street. He was followed by Jedediah Budd. Raider stood transfixed with horror. Up till this, he had been bored, grouchy, with a sore gut. He could live with that. But not with this! Not Huggins!

The newly arrived Pinkerton agent, appearing well fed and pleased with himself, looked around him in a benevolent way. He spotted Raider and strode toward him, his hand extended, a smile on his chubby face.

Raider turned his back and headed in a hurry toward the batwing doors of the First and Last.

Orville Huggins looked puzzled and insulted. "There must be some mistake. Surely Raider remembers me—"

The wily old miner Jedediah Budd put a restraining hand on Orville's arm to stop him from following Raider into the saloon. "He remembers you, Orville. Let him be. He needs a little time to let it soak in."

• • •

In the chain of hills between Hugoton and Coronado, springs gave birth to tiny streams which joined into large streams as they traveled downhill. These watercourses were lined with small trees—wild plum, currant, chokecherry, with wild grapevines twining through them. The streamside meadows sported violets, buttercups, blue and white daisies, goldenrod, and bluish-purple patches of poison flowering locoweed. The streams occasionally widened into pools, hidden by thickets. Charlene and Doc had their favorite picnic place, at one of these hidden pools. It was their secret oasis in the flat sameness of the prairies.

Charlene and Doc had finished their picnic lunch and were lying in the shade of a wild plum tree, listening to the trickling stream enter the pool and the song of a small bird that hopped around in the undergrowth. Doc was inclined to doze, and each time he did so, Charlene tickled his nose with a stalk of grass. She seemed to have something on her mind.

Doc guessed what it was she had on her mind when her fingers strayed inside his shirt and wandered over his chest. But when he rolled onto his side to hold her to him, she pulled back out of his reach. When he stretched a hand farther to touch her, she backed off more. Doc raised himself on one knee, and she jumped to her feet. She hiked up her prairie dress around her knees and ran off through the meadow grass. She looked back over one shoulder to see if he was coming after her.

Doc was. She looked back once more, than ran as fast as she could through the grass, encumbered by her long dress.

She stopped suddenly and pointed. "A snake!" she screamed.

Doc stooped, grabbed a rock, and scanned the grass for movement.

She ran on and called back, "Fooled you!"

This time Doc went after her in earnest. He allowed her to stay a little ahead of him until she arrived back at the bank of the stream. He grabbed her there, closed his arms about her, and sank with her to the grass.

"Someone help me!" Charlene cried out. In an undertone she added, "Be my hard luck someone might hear me and come stop you."

Doc laughed and held her to him. He kissed her and ran his lips down her neck.

She eased out of his arms and said, "I want to swim."

"So take off your clothes."

"You first."

They teased each other like a pair of innocents until Doc stripped naked, waded into the pool, and promised not to look while Charlene undressed.

He dived into the cold clear water, surfaced, and wiped the wet hair out of his eyes to watch her as she came running naked through the grass toward the water. She hesitated on the bank, among the trees, before entering the water. Standing there with one arm in front of her breasts and a hand held modestly before her pubic hair, she reminded Doc of a nymph in a Greek myth.

They splashed around in the water together and forgot the entire world beyond their stream pool until they heard one of their horses whinny. Doc climbed out of the water to take a look, while Charlene immersed herself in water up to the neck, forgetting that the crystal clear water wouldn't conceal her very much anyway.

"Two horsemen," Doc said. "They've spotted our horses, but they're heading up into the hills in a hurry. You want me to holler for them to come here for a swim?"

"Doc, don't you dare. I'd never forgive you."

He waited till the two horsemen had disappeared from

sight and then helped Charlene out of the pool. They lay on the grass and the sun dried the water droplets on their skins.

Doc licked the last of the stream water from Charlene's neck and shoulders. Her breathing became heavy, and she began to press her soft body against his. Doc ran his hand gently across one breast, brushing the nipple with his fingertips, and slowly continued down to her narrowing waist, over the rise of her hip, around her smooth rounded buttock and over her silky thigh. She opened her legs and thrust her lower belly toward him. She moaned with pleasure when she felt the tip of his enlarged member touch the moist swelling lips of her sex.

She reached down and guided him into her, but only a little way, teasingly. She held his face in her hands and kissed him hard and long, thrusting her tongue between his lips.

He could feel her warm cunt squeezing and tugging on his shaft. He rolled her onto her back and slid all the way into her. She parted her legs as wide as she could, and he drove in an inch deeper.

Her eyes were shut and she was making low groans in time to the rhythmic movements of her hips beneath him, as he delved into her with long strokes of his bulging manhood.

The two horsemen who had spotted Doc and Charlene's mounts tied among the small trees at the stream had by now reached the crest of the hills, and they saw Coronado ahead of them across the grassy plains.

"I appreciate your coming along with me," Orville Huggins told Jedediah Budd.

"Raider's going to be mad enough at me for not telling him what you're up to, but he'd have my hide if I let you go alone and kept my mouth shut."

Orville shook his head. "I can't understand Raider's at-titude to me. I know he must blame me for taking the wrong train up in Nevada and for all the delay and confusion in my getting here. And he has a right to be mad at me about that. I was his partner and I should have stuck by his side, come hell or high water. Instead, I took a train in the wrong direction." Orville sighed regretfully. "Now I must prove myself worthy to be his partner. You know, Jed, Raider once trusted and depended on me."

Budd tried to smother his laugh.

Orville was too preoccupied to notice. "And then there's Doc Weatherbee. I bet that right now Doc is out laying some trap for Lyman or scouting the lay of the land so he can spring some surprise on him. Doc's a legendary operative—I've always dreamed of working with him one day. We've never met, and I'm sure he's never even heard of me—unless Raider has told him bad things about me. That would be all the more reason why I should make a strong first impression on him. Jed, I intend to prove to both of them that I am as highly competent in the field as they. And you'll have guessed how I intend to prove that to them. You're right! By bringing in the man they couldn't lay hands on. Today I'm going to bring back Myles Lyman to Hugoton, dead or alive!"

Budd nodded uneasily and looked into the far distance. He was sorry now he had told Orville anything. Raider had refused to give Huggins details of the case, and it was Budd who heard what happened over a few whiskies with Mad Mike at the First and Last. Jedediah and Mad Mike had been bumping into each other in four states for more than twenty years. They recalled the bad old days when things were really rough and a man had to be a real man to survive out west and not like a lot of the dudes and weaklings the train was bringing in now. Only places these days that were free of these slickers were those that could be reached only by burro on a mountain path. Which reminded Budd again that he had no place as a miner on the prairies. He hadn't been down on the Great Plains for so long that he'd forgotten it existed, and he reckoned he hadn't been missing much either. In another day or two he'd cross over into Colorado and head west for the San Juan Mountains, where there was talk of big gold and silver strikes. Only trouble was, by now he was feeling kind of responsible for Orville.

They rode together over the flat grassland to Coronado, and as they neared the town, Budd grew more apprehensive and Huggins more confident.

"What you got in mind for us to do, Orville? I mean, they ain't hardly going to let you ride in, grab Lyman, and ride out again. Mad Mike told me Lyman has confederates in this town."

"Leave it to me," Orville said.

Budd was not fooled. "Ain't you got nothing worked out in your mind about what you're going to do when you find him?"

"Too much planning makes a man rigid and unre-sponsive, Jed. Better to go with the flow, think on the move—"

"—die in your boots," Budd finished the sentence for him.

"I'd have thought you would have learned by now to trust in my judgment," Orville said in an offended tone.

Budd shook his head sadly and crossed himself. He would say no more.

When they rode down the main street of Coronado, no one paid them much heed.

"No one knows me here," Orville said. "You got nothing to worry about. Nothing happens until we set things in motion. Look, there's the Plain Hell saloon. I'll buy you a drink."

They hitched their horses to the rail outside. Both tried not to look at Myles Lyman, whom they recognized immediately from Mad Mike's description and who was sitting by himself at a table just inside the door. There were fewer than a dozen men in the saloon, some just lingering, a few throwing back whiskey in earnest while standing at the bar.

Orville and Jedediah had a bottle of redeye placed between them and they helped themselves into none-too-clean chipped glasses. Budd waited a while for Huggins to do something and then got tired of waiting and talked to a big Southerner standing next to him at the bar. When the man turned to face him, Budd saw he was wearing a marshal's badge. He went right on talking to him, trying to get Orville involved in the conversation also so that he would see the lawman's badge. But Orville was too busy in his own mind setting up his plan of action. He wouldn't pay any attention, no matter how urgently Budd tugged on his arm.

Then Orville Huggins sprang into action. A number of long strides took him over next to the table at which Lyman sat. Orville whipped out his revolver and covered Lyman.

"I got some people who want to talk with you, fella," Orville rasped in a tone of voice Budd had never heard him use before. "Now, git on your feet before my finger gets itchy and let your gun fall on the floor."

Jedediah Budd saw the harmless-looking consumptive youth leaning against a wall nearby give the marshal a look and ease back his suit coat to uncover the handle of a six-gun. Before the marshal could signal a reply, Budd slapped his hands on top of the bar counter to show he was not thinking about drawing his own gun and said quickly, "That man is a Pinkerton, sent here to arrest Lyman. It wouldn't be wise for you to give the signal to kill him."

The big man thought fast. He just looked at the youth over by the wall, and the youth let his suit coat fall back to cover the gun handle again. Meanwhile Orville was threatening Lyman in his weird new voice and waving his gun in his face. The sick-looking young man picked up an empty bottle with a candle stub in its neck and batted Orville over the head with it. The Pinkerton's knees wobbled, and he sank to the floor with a surprised look on his face.

"You a Pinkerton too?" the marshal asked Budd.

"Hell, no. I'm a miner. Name's Jedediah Budd."

"I'm Turk Calhoun."

They shook hands.

Turk nodded at Orville's prone figure on the floor. "This boy come over from Hugoton?"

"That's right."

"I thought so. Well, you better take him right back there. We got no use for him here."

"Sure, Turk. Only he's a mite heavier than I am, and I'm not as young as I used to be. I'd appreciate a hand in tying him across his saddle."

Turk grunted like he was annoyed, but he walked across to where Orville was lying near the door. In a single easy motion, he reached down, threw Orville across one shoulder, and went out the door. He heaved him like a dead man across his saddle, and Budd took some time to tie Orville's wrists to his ankles beneath the horse's belly, so he wouldn't slip off.

"Budd." It was Turk Calhoun at the door of the saloon again. He handed Jedediah the bottle of redeye he had been drinking from inside, with the cork loosely pressed into its neck. "Listen to me careful now, miner. You get back in them thar gold-bearing hills quick as you can. You don't belong down here."

"Sure thing, Turk."

By the time they reached Hugoton three hours later, Orville was still groggy but was able to sit upright in the saddle, so that at least his dignity was saved.

He said to Budd, "I was thinking it might be best not to mention what went on today. What do you think?"

Budd grinned. "I thought you were a stickler for regulations and reports, Orville."

Huggins looked offended. "Of course I'll mention it in my next report to Chicago, but there I can dismiss it as 'an unsuccessful attempt' or use words to that effect without going into embarrassing details."

"I won't say nothing, Orville." Budd was beginning to feel a longing for a pickax and the side of a mountain, and this time it wasn't just gold fever pushing him there.

"It's high time you leveled with me," Turk Calhoun told Myles Lyman in Lyman's room at the Bluestem Hotel. "Pour us another drink, Snead, if you will. Now, I find what you say to be real interesting, and I think I might guess that Snead does too. You misjudge us, Lyman, when you think we would have no interest in an ongoing business such as the one you plan here in Coronado. Only one thing upsets me in what you have been telling me."

Myles looked nervous. "What's that?"

"You keep talking about yourself hiring this one to do that and that one to do something else. You'll give them this or that. But what I don't hear you talking about is taking on partners."

"I didn't think you'd be interested, " Myles said evasively.

"We are."

Myles turned to Snead. "You too?"

"What he says," Snead snapped.

"Very well, then. That certainly changes things. I'll think

over what terms to offer you and let you know——"

"No deal, Lyman," Turk said. "We'll be the ones to offer you terms. Equal partners, a third each, I say."

"But that would leave you two more than me," Myles said, plainly disturbed. "I'll give you a half share and I keep the other half. You two split your half share any way you please."

"Agreed."

Calhoun surprised Lyman by his easy acceptance, until he remembered that some Southerners considered it beneath them to haggle.

"All right, number one, we give you protection against these damn Pinkertons and anyone else who comes along," Turk summed up, holding up his glass for Snead to fill. "Number two, we take care of Hugoton as a rival town to Coronado. You should have brought us in on this deal earlier on, Myles. Before this, our hearts weren't in our work."

"I thought I could do it alone," Myles confessed. "It took that goddamn stupid Pinkerton today to teach me I couldn't. Now I feel greatly relieved. I got no concerns now about my personal safety with you two as my partners. But I still have big worries about Hugoton. Lynch and Murdock have been doing more and more cattle buying. It's gotten to the point now that word's out along the Chisholm Trail that it's good to veer over in Hugoton's direction for a chance to sell off the herd there and take a week or more off the journey without sacrificing a dollar in price. You see what Lynch and Murdock are doing? They're setting a precedent, as the lawyers say. By the time the railroads get down this way, they will already have set up Hugoton as a buying center while Coronado will still be a nothing town. Any railroadman in his right senses is going to lay track toward an established market instead of trying to build a new one. We could still lose our railroad to Hugoton, even if ours wins the race to get here first and collect the government grants. The government don't care whether it's to Coronado or Hugoton. It's all the same to outsiders—they'll pick the easy way."

Myles rose from his chair and agitatedly pointed out the hotel room window. "See that dust on the horizon. I bet Murdock and Lynch buy that herd. You know what I been reduced to? Riding out to meet the trail bosses to try to persuade them Hugoton is a crooked town. Doesn't work. We got to think of something."

Turk Calhoun ambled over to the window and looked at the distant dust cloud for a while. Then he said to Snead, "Round up five or six of those drifters who came into town this morning. Make sure none of them came by way of Hugoton, and offer them twenty dollars each in gold for a day's work. They'll know what you mean."

Calhoun, Snead, and Lyman waited on horseback behind a small bluff in the grassland between the herd and Hugoton. Turk waited till they saw a group of riders approach from Hugoton before explaining things to Lyman.

"Seven," Snead counted. "Our five men plus two others."

"Murdock and Lynch, if we're in luck," Turk said with a grin. "Now, Myles, you get to do your duty. We sent those men into Hugoton to claim they were cowhands with that herd yonder. We told them to bring Murdock and Lynch out to meet the trail boss and see the cows. Is that them?"

Myles looked carefully. "It's them. Now's your chance."

Turk grinned again. "As partners along with you, Myles, Snead and I agreed we'd let you get your hands dirty with this one."

"Me? Not me!" Myles said indignantly. "I hired you—"

"You didn't hire me, Myles," Calhoun said playfully.

"I'm your partner, and I'm sitting here waiting for you to do your bit."

Turk reached across and drew Lyman's Winchester repeating rifle from its saddle sheath. He levered a shell into the firing chamber and handed it to Myles.

"I'm a lousy shot," Myles claimed.

"Then keep shooting till you hit them," Turk told him, and there was now an edge of command and menace in his voice which was not lost on Myles.

Lyman raised the rifle to his shoulder, sighted along the barrel, and squeezed the trigger.

Tom Murdock pitched forward from his horse and fell to the ground.

Myles looked unable to believe what he had done. He laid the rifle crosswise on the saddle.

"Replace the shell!" Calhoun barked. After Myles dazedly obeyed him by levering another shell into the chamber, he commanded, "Get the other one!"

Myles fired and missed. Calhoun yelled. Myles fired and missed again.

Rob Lynch had turned his horse about. He now was riding low in the saddle and eating up the ground on the way back to Hugoton.

Turk nodded to Snead.

Snead pulled out his rifle, eased a shell in place, and unhurriedly, with one shot, blew Lynch out of the saddle.

CHAPTER ELEVEN

The bodies of Tom Murdock and Rob Lynch were recovered less than an hour after they died. When a posse rode out of Hugoton to confront the cowhands riding with the herd, they found none of the five men who had claimed to be riding with this herd, and the trail boss told them he had meant to stop in at Hugoton but had sent none of his men and was missing none now. Naturally the Hugoton posse got around to thinking about Coronado, but it was nearing sundown and there wasn't much they could do till the next day, except stop off at the saloons and cuss and say what they were going to do.

Murdock and Lynch were buried early next morning, a humid, overcast day without a breath of air stirring. After the short ceremony at the graveyard, the men came back to the saloons and there was more cussing and threatening at Coronado. Everyone wondered what Mad Mike and the Kid were up to. All anyone knew was they had saddled up at the stables before first light and ridden out. Toward Coronado, some reckoned. Toward Texas, others said.

Doc Weatherbee and Raider were offering sympathy but keeping out of the fighting talk. Orville Huggins was very quiet, not sure if his misadventure had any connection with the subsequent murder of the two cattle dealers, yet suspecting it had in some way unknown to him. Jedediah Budd was raring to go back to the goldfields, but he couldn't quite bring himself to leave just yet, in spite of Turk Calhoun's warning to him, until he had seen what was going to happen.

Mad Mike and the Kid got back in town early. They had a bound and bleeding man on a horse the Kid was leading.

Mike said, "We figured these fellas who lured Murdock and Lynch would collect their pay and skip first thing this morning, so me and the Kid took ourselves over near Coronado before day was properly up. We ran down two of 'em—that's the surviving one you see there. His buddy died of persuasion 'cause he was slow to tell his story. We brought this one back so y'all could hear him talk. And he's a real good talker when he's prompted right, ain't he, Kid?"

The Kid pushed the man out of the saddle so he fell headlong onto the dust, hands bound behind his back. Then the Kid dismounted and drew his bowie knife. The bound man began whimpering and squealing when he saw the Kid approach him with the blade. The Kid just laughed and cut him free of his bonds. The man lay where he was, rubbing his wrists.

"Git up!" the Kid snarled and darted the tip of the bowie into his chest.

The man howled but staggered to his feet quick as he could.

"Talk!" the Kid said, never one for wasting words. He gave the man another jab with the blade, this time in the upper arm. The man's shirt sleeve had already been ripped off, and everyone could see the puncture wound made by the big bowie start to leak blood, which dripped off his arm at the elbow.

In a hoarse quavering voice, the man began to talk.

It hadn't taken much to work up the Hugoton mob. Few of them had had a good word to say for either Rob Lynch or Tom Murdock while they were still alive, but now they claimed they were willing to ride to the ends of the earth to avenge their deaths. With all three of the big cattle dealers gone, the townspeople realized that a major blow had been struck against the town of Hugoton and that they had better strike back. They were open to suggestions. The Kid had a few.

"Let's string up this belly-crawling snake in the grass."

The crowd roared its approval.

"I didn't do no killing," the man whined. "All I took was twenty dollars to lead two men out to the herd. None of us fired a shot. It was Lyman and Calhoun and Snead. Not us."

The crowd listened quietly to his complaints. They were enjoying this. They knew what they were going to do, and letting their victim blabber on like this was almost the same as giving him a trial with them as the jury. So they listened, and he pleaded and offered to lure Lyman right into the middle of Hugoton for them. The Kid and the others even pretended to go along with this for a while. When they got tired of this, they fetched a rope.

Doc Weatherbee stepped in. "You can't hang this man without a trial. Mike, it's up to you, as marshal of this town, to ensure that law and order are maintained. I'll see to it that you'll be held responsible if you permit this man to be lynched."

Mad Mike nodded to Doc and said to the Kid, "The Pinkerton is right. The judge will be in town next week. I don't want this man hung in the meantime. Kid, you and these folk conduct him to a cell while me, Doc, and these gents have ourselves a drink at the First and Last."

Doc saw him wink at the Kid, but there wasn't much he could say about that. As they went into the saloon, Doc looked back and saw the Kid and some of the others stomping the prisoner. Doc knew the man would never reach the town cells alive, but there wasn't much he could do about that either. Like the marshal said, he didn't want this man hung.

"You coming with us to Coronado?" Mad Mike asked inside the saloon. "We ride out in a short time."

"Great!" Raider exclaimed.

"Certainly not!" Doc Weatherbee said sharply. "We're Pinkertons, and we can't get involved in your town war. That's not just my opinion. Regulations are very firm on this."

"Absolutely," Orville Huggins agreed.

"So you're just going to sit this one out while we go after Lyman for you?" Mad Mike taunted.

"You're going after Lyman for murder now," Doc replied. "We only had conspiracy to commit arson on him. Your charge is the one to press."

"We may hang him," Mad Mike said.

"He certainly deserves it more than the unfortunate who is being kicked to death on the street right now. Marshal, the people here may like the way you run this town. I don't. I'm not your friend."

Mike nodded to Doc. "Say it like it is, Weatherbee. All right then, I take it you got no objections if Lyman happens to get stood on by my horse or meets some other tragic accident when we go to kick ass in Coronado."

Doc shrugged. "What makes you think you're going to be doing anything in Coronado except ducking bullets as you try to get near the place?"

That stopped Mad Mike. After a pause, he said, "I guess we was planning to make a wild charge and take the place by storm."

"Half of you will be picked off by rifles," Doc observed casually, as if this might not be a bad thing at all.

"I suppose, Doc, if you were to take a group of men against Coronado, you'd do it differently."

"I would."

Mike smiled and poured Doc a drink from the bottle. "For the purposes of conversation only, I wouldn't mind hearing how you would go about it."

Doc told him.

The rich widows of Murdock and Lynch said they would be pleased to contribute $250 each in gold to finance vengeance on their husbands' killers. They went with Mad Mike to the Hugoton bank, where he filled a canvas bag with $500 in gold coins before the eyes of a score of townspeople. These men rode with Mike out to the trail boss of the herd, which had now passed the town and gone through a gap in the chain of low hills. The trail boss had never heard of such an offer in his life before, and he'd heard of some strange stories in his time.

"You want to *hire* my cattle, not buy them?"

"That's what I said," Mike told him. "You got less than two thousand head. You'd get less than two thousand dollars for the entire herd at a stockyard. I'm offering to rent these cows from you for five hundred dollars for only a few hours. You may have a few beasts killed, and the others may lose a few pounds, but what the hell do you care since you got

ive hundred in gold in your saddlebag before I drive a
ingle steer."

"How do I know I'm going to get my herd back?" the
rail boss asked.

"Because you and your men are coming with us on this
rive."

The drover talked some more about strange deals until
Mike showed him the gold coins inside the canvas bag.
They shook hands on the deal and got the herd under way.

They were no more than five miles from Coronado at
he time, with only flat grassland between them and the
own. They had twelve cowhands and maybe forty men
rom Hugoton, more than enough horsemen to steer the herd
recisely. The longhorns were kept moving at a fast lick till
hey were about a mile outside Coronado. Then the riders
mptied their six-guns in the air and whooped. The steers
anicked and tried to run this way and that, but the numerous
orsemen stampeded them in a thick bunch right at the main
treet of Coronado.

No one wasted their time in the town firing on this ad-
ancing tide of horns and hooves. The steers swarmed into
he main street, crushed each other against buildings, snap-
ing down porch supports, destroying sidewalks, demo-
ishing wagons, sweeping all in their way. The people of
ne town had ample time to see what was bearing down on
nem, and they had all rushed into the houses and cabins,
vhere they waited, peering out windows and doorways with
neir rifles ready.

But the riders driving the stampede through town did not
ollow it through the main street. While the horde of long-
orns was wrecking everything but solid buildings, the rid-
rs passed along either side of the town and shot in through
ack windows and doors. They picked men off the roofs.
hey shot at shadowy figures inside windows. And when

they saw no particular human target to aim at, they emptied
their rifles anyplace they thought someone might be taking
shelter.

The herd passed through the town and onto the grassland
on the other side, where the riders slowed it down. Mad
Mike signaled he wanted the herd turned around for another
run through the town. They hadn't lost a single man and
had inflicted high casualties and much damage.

As the herd was being driven for the first time toward
Coronado, Myles Lyman, Turk Calhoun, and Snead rushed
out of the livery stables where they were about to unsaddle
their horses. Calhoun took in the situation instantly and
barked at the other two in his military way to follow him.
The three men fetched their mounts and rode out of town
in a clatter of hooves, well ahead of the herd. While the
cows stampeded through Coronado and the riders fired on
the houses, Calhoun, Lyman, and Snead circled around at
a distance and rode for the hills.

"Did you see the Pinkertons there?" Turk yelled to Myles.

"I saw them!" he shouted back. Myles had been seeing
Pinkertons everywhere he looked, even in his sleep.

Turk was satisfied. "Good! We're going to teach them
and all those Hugoton boys a lesson."

They climbed into the line of low hills, from the crest
of which they would be able to see Hugoton. It was a little
after midday, and the leaden skies hung low over the prairie
and lower still over the hills. Sweat poured from all three
men just from the effort of sitting in the saddle. From time
to time, Turk mopped dry the palm and fingers of his gun
hand. Snead was sweating inside his greasy suit, but he
didn't take off the coat or even loosen the collar. He looked
more deathly pale than usual, and Myles noticed how clearly

the blue veins ran beneath his white skin. Myles himself was a bit hung over. He had celebrated the passing on of his two rivals, Murdock and Lynch, till the early morning hours and drowned whatever guilt he had over his having killed one of them himself. He didn't want to have to do that again.

Drinking the champagne, Myles had told himself that Hugoton was now nothing. He was king! Today it wasn't quite working out like that. Myles couldn't help noticing that it was Turk, not him, who was giving the orders—and not even bothering to explain them. Why were they going to Hugoton? Without Murdock and Lynch, the town was no longer a serious threat to Coronado. Why bother teaching its people a lesson? They would learn soon enough when they saw their town wither away while Coronado prospered. Yet he instinctively felt that now was not the right time to confront Calhoun with his own wishes. It galled Myles Lyman to have to do what he was told by someone else.

They reached the top of the hills and saw Hugoton ahead, looking still and empty under the gray clouds.

"I'll wait," Snead said.

"Sure," Turk agreed.

Myles was alarmed. "Why isn't he coming with us?"

"He'll catch up," Turk said. "You come with me."

This was too much! Myles bristled. "Damn it, Turk, stop treating me like a child or a servant. If you expect me to treat you as an equal partner, you'd better treat me likewise. And that includes a few words of explanation when you want me to go along with your decisions."

Calhoun nodded, not put out in the least. "I thought you'd have noticed by now."

"Noticed? Noticed what?"

"That we were being followed."

"Followed!" Myles twisted about in the saddle to look behind, but they had crossed over the crest of the hills and he could see no one, except Snead standing next to his horse behind a big rock. "Who's following us? Why didn't you mention this before?"

"I said nothing in case you'd twist around in the saddle like you just did and let him know we'd cottoned on to him." Calhoun was talking to him like he was a child or a simpleton. "You want to know who it is. It's just one man alone. I think it's the Kid."

"Oh, my God."

"Snead will take care of him."

"That's what you think!" Myles shouted, panicked. "I've seen the Kid in action. He'll kill Snead easy."

Turk shrugged one shoulder. "Then I guess I'll take him. And if the Kid kills me, I guess you can nail him to revenge us both."

Myles smiled wanly. "Sure thing, Turk."

Calhoun laughed.

The Kid didn't come over the crest of the hills where Snead expected him to, but nearly a quarter of a mile off to the west. It was obvious the Kid knew he must have been spotted as he followed them across the open grassland and took a different route up the hills so he couldn't be bush-wacked by a rifleman. He was standing next to some rocks now, looking at Calhoun and Lyman riding on toward Hugoton and wondering where the third horseman had hidden himself. Snead mounted his horse, and the Kid saw him right away.

Instead of riding down the slope after the other two, Snead crossed the ridge toward the Kid. The Kid waited, standing beside his horse.

While Snead was still a hundred yards away, they started

staring each other down, seeing who would break first. These two had nothing to say to each other, and both knew it.

When Snead was maybe thirty feet off, the Kid dropped his eyes suddenly to the saddle blanket draped across the base of the neck of Snead's horse. He went for his six-gun. Snead lifted the blanket high enough so the barrel of the sawed-off American Arms 12-gauge shotgun cleared his horse's hide. He pulled on the trigger.

The blanket billowed out before the muzzle of the shotgun and the load of shot covered the Kid from the waist up and took him off his feet. The lead shot buried itself deep in his flesh, ripping raw his face, chest, and arms.

Snead didn't bother to finish him off and left him to die on the hilltop beneath the threatening clouds.

"Looks almost like a ghost town," Myles Lyman observed as he, Calhoun, and Snead neared Hugoton. "Not a soul stirring. What're we going to do, Turk?" He nearly bit his tongue in frustration. Here he was asking for orders!

"Shoot the place up, I reckon," Turk answered him back vaguely.

"I know what we should do," Myles announced.

Calhoun and Snead glanced at him in surprise.

"Rob the Western National Bank!"

Turk said, "Not bad, Myles. If we can ride into town and not get shot at, mebbe we will."

Myles went on, excited now that he could see some material gain in this expedition. "The manager, if he ain't at the bank, will be in the First and Last saloon. If he ain't there, he'll be at home, just a few houses away down the main street. That poor bastard will take one look at you guys, quake in his boots, and hand over the keys to the safe."

No one shot at them, and they saw no one as they rode into town. The bank was closed.

"They're coming this way!" Orville Huggins announced in a nervous stage whisper and drew back from the front window of the First and Last.

"Seems like you got some customers out there," Raider told the bank manager, who was spilling whiskey from the glass in his trembling hand and backing off toward the wall farthest from the door.

Orville sat at a table with Jedediah Budd, trying to calm himself. The barkeep got ready to duck beneath his counter. No one else was in the place except Doc Weatherbee, who was too busy lighting one of his Old Virginia cheroots to bother with what was going on. Doc's unconcern secretly infuriated Raider, especially since he knew that Doc in all likelihood was unarmed and totally confident he could handle everything with words.

Calhoun came in first through the batwing doors, followed by Snead and lastly Lyman. Myles stood just inside the doors, instantly transfixed with terror when he saw the Pinkertons. Snead went to the nearest wall and leaned against it, looking tired and sick. Turk never batted an eye, walked right in, and faced Raider at the bar.

"I thought you boys would be playing buckaroo with them steers over in Coronado," he said in a friendly tone.

It was Doc who answered him. "We don't concern ourselves with the differences between these two towns, Mr. Calhoun. Neither have we anything against you or your associate, Mr. Snead. I can't say that for the rest of Hugoton's residents, though. It may be unsafe for you here when they return."

"So they left you in charge while they were gone." Turk was speaking to Doc but watching Raider.

"We're taking care of the women, children, and valuables," Doc agreed. "We've been watching you ride in and let you come because we're anxious to talk with Mr. Lyman. Would you care for a drink, Mr. Calhoun?"

Doc was at his smoothest and most casual. Even Raider had to admit that Weatherbee was unnerving the big Southerner.

"No, we got to push on," Turk said.

"I'm afraid we must ask you to leave Mr. Lyman behind," Doc said in a very cold, precise, polite voice.

The atmosphere in the saloon was only tense before. Now it was electric.

"He comes with us," Turk growled, watching Raider's eyes.

"I'm afraid we can't permit that," Doc said, in a voice like a sexton telling someone to put out a cigarette in church.

Turk looked slowly and unhurriedly about him, taking everything in, weighing all the chances. His gaze settled on Jedediah Budd, sitting at the table with Orville. "So you're still here, miner. I told you once to head for the hills. Remember?"

Budd was visibly terrified. As soon as Calhoun's gaze moved on, Budd drew his six-gun surreptitiously, cocked it, and held it hidden beneath the table. He did not mistake the look Calhoun had given him—if Calhoun took Raider, Budd was a dead man. Budd watched Snead, the harmless-looking consumptive, lounging against the wall. Budd watched him like he would a rattlesnake.

Calhoun was not first to go for his gun. It was Snead—out of Raider's clear line of vision but with a clean shot at him. Budd aimed beneath the table and squeezed the trigger. Snead crumpled.

Raider and Turk both went for their guns at the same instant. Turk was no match for the Pinkerton. Raider fanned off a shot, and the slug caught Turk in the chest. He hit the floorboards with the force of a falling tree.

They checked both of them. Calhoun and Snead had both died as they lived—by the gun.

Doc was the first to notice. "Where's Myles Lyman?"

Raider, Doc Weatherbee, Orville Huggins, and Jedediah Budd left for Coronado later that afternoon. Great thunderheads were piling up in the sky all about them. They meant to put Myles Lyman under arrest and charge him with murder, among other things, and if possible make peace between the two towns now that most of the major trouble-makers in both places were dead.

Lyman must have slipped out the batwing doors, or under them, when gunfire broke out in the First and Last. His horse was hitched to the rail outside the bank, and he took Calhoun and Snead's mounts with him. By the time any of the Pinkertons could have run to the stable and saddled a horse to go after him, Lyman would have built too much of a lead to be caught. It had been an oversight on the part of the Pinkertons in not having horses ready. They hadn't thought they might have to leave town in a hurry—but they were making no excuses. Myles Lyman had outmaneuvered them and was free again.

The Hugoton townsmen returned shortly afterward. Besides the corpse of the Kid, which they discovered on the way back, they had suffered no losses. Three men had been injured, none seriously.

Mad Mike told Raider and Doc, "After we turned the herd around and ran it through the town a second time, I was ready to go in and wreck the place. But not these cowards. They knew there were men with guns in those houses waiting on them. They'd send the cattle in and fire from a distance, but, hell, they wouldn't come in closer

than that. I looked around for the Kid to help me rouse
some support for an attack and could find neither hide nor
hair of him. I had no way of knowing he was already
following Calhoun and the others. So everything just kind
of petered out and we all came home. Yeah, sure we saw
Myles Lyman. It wasn't long after we'd picked up the Kid's
body and had come down on this side of the hills. I was
feeling mighty upset, and the fight was knocked out of me
for a spell. I didn't have the heart to chase after Lyman
myself, and the rest of the men were tired and their horses
were wore down after driving that herd and whatnot. I'd
have to tell you we let him go. He was heading for Coronado
at a fast lick."

"Sorry about the Kid," Doc said.

"Well, you boys took out Calhoun and Snead, so that
evens the score," Mad Mike said. "I'm sure sorry now I
didn't go after Lyman—I just never connected him with the
Kid's death somehow." He shook his head. "If you boys
are going after him—and I know you are—I 'spect he'll
stay the night at Coronado and head out first light tomorrow.
You're going to have to lay hands on him before that."

The Pinkertons saddled up and left right away. They
climbed over the ridge of low hills. Coronado lay across
the grassland. Off on the horizon, the herd was moving
north and raising huge clouds of dust. But today the dust
clouds were nothing compared with the thunderclouds overhead. All day the sky had been gray, overcast, unmoving,
hot, humid, with not enough air to move a blade of grass.
Now things were changing. Strong gusts came out of nowhere and just as suddenly died down. Again the winds
would come from another direction and disappear in a few
minutes. Instead of being in an even gray layer as before,
the clouds now were tumbling, traveling fast, and forming
all kinds of fantastic shapes.

Off to their left, a huge anvil-shaped thunderhead moved across the sky. Shafts of rain fell from its smooth leaden bottom. To their right, clouds were piled so high on a thunderhead they looked like scoops of gray pudding slopped on top of each other by a child. A fast eerie wind whistled over the empty grassland.

Orville busied himself with pulling a poncho out of a saddlebag and keeping it ready for use, looking worriedly up at the more threatening clouds. The others just ignored the weather, including Doc, who Orville thought should be worried about his worsted wool suit.

Then very quickly the big thunderhead that had been to their left passed over their heads. It was very dark under the cloud, and its dense black ceiling stretched for miles. In spite of the heat and humidity, hail began to fall. The stones were big as dimes, some big as quarters, and the four horsemen took a battering, glad of their hats to protect their heads.

The hail stopped, and once again they could see about them. The black cloud seemed to have dropped almost to touch the grass directly in front of them. There was no sound except for their horses' hooves crushing the hailstones on the ground. Raider reined in his horse and looked at the boiling cloud in front of them, now shot through with beams of light which gave the roiling mist an unearthly gray-pink glow. The others stopped alongside him and no one said anything.

Raider pointed.

A funnel reached from the earth up into the huge dark cloud. The funnel itself was monstrously big and looked as if it was made of dense black fluid. It moved diagonally across their path, and they saw jets of dust leap up into it and scissor around it. The funnel was larger than they imagined any moving thing could be, and it glided along in an impossible silence.

The four horsemen sat without moving, helpless before the immense forces of nature. The funnel passed before their eyes, directly across their path. Then it lifted off the ground and vanished into the looming cloud overhead. A shaft of sunlight broke through at a place where the clouds were torn apart and lit swirls of red dust that were blowing across the grassland in the hot dark afternoon.

They saw another funnel grow from the cloud, but it didn't touch down on the ground and quickly dissipated. All at once three funnels touched down just on the near side of Coronado, twisted around each other like square dancers, and struck the town.

Myles Lyman was in his room at the Bluestem Hotel, packing his trunk. He planned to get everything ready to leave at dawn and had already hired a wagon, a driver, and a man to ride shotgun. He'd leave his gold in the town bank till morning for safekeeping and collect it as he left town. He'd go to Wichita and from there to Topeka and hopefully straighten out the bond mess now that Murdock and the others were no longer around to threaten sellers and buyers. In a few months he would pay a visit to Coronado again to see what opportunities there might be.

He put two shirts into the trunk and stood to listen. He could hear a high-pitched whirring noise that was increasing in volume alarmingly, but he couldn't detect its source. Looking out the window from the top floor of the two-story hotel, he saw people in the street running and their hats being whipped from their heads by wind. Then the glass panes rattled so loudly Myles stepped back into the room, away from the window. He sat on the edge of the bed, badly frightened by the immense whirling scream of sound that seemed to come from every direction.

The entire hotel building began to rock. Suddenly the air in the room grew cold.

He looked up. He couldn't believe his eyes. The whole roof had been lifted off the big hotel like a lid off a pot, and the ceiling of his room was now hovering two feet above the four walls with air rushing in the gap between.

Everything disintegrated. Timber boards scattered like feathers. Myles was repeatedly struck by flying objects before he felt that he too was being lifted up into the terrible jaws of this roaring monster.

Enmities forgotten, the Hugoton folk worked night and day, ferrying the wounded from the broken shell of Coronado to their town, sheltering the homeless, feeding the hungry, and comforting those in mourning. They collected the smashed timber in wagons and hauled it to Hugoton to build cabins for those who wanted to stay, and most did. But there was no talk of rebuilding Coronado. There was only one town now, and that was Hugoton. Folks now considered Coronado unlucky, and while no one, except for a few, was saying that the finger of God had directed the tornadoes to hit Coronado, no one wanted to go back there again to test out if the place was really cursed. That was already history. They were in Hugoton now.

Farmers from the settlement had come to help. Three of them found Myles Lyman, still alive but with no hope of ever walking again, so the doctor said after carefully examining him.

"I might believe that about another man," Raider responded, "but I'm keeping an eye on this critter. While you got your eye on him he'll by lying here close to dying, but you turn your back a moment and he'll be galloping outa town on a stolen horse."

Myles chuckled under the blanket. "Naw, not this time, Raider. But you're right when you say I'm going to cheat all you lawmen again—but this time it's only going to be by dying on you before you can get me in that courtroom."

"Maybe we'll lynch you, then, while we still got the chance," Raider said.

Myles smiled sadly. "You'll want to hurry it on. I got the feeling I'm slipping away fast."

The Eagle Hotel had been converted into a hospital, and Myles Lyman lay on a mattress on the floor of the dining room with fifteen others.

He next insisted that Doc Weatherbee fetch a pen and paper because he wanted to make a will. He sent Raider in search of the three farmers who had found him, Charlene, Mad Mike, Huggins, and Budd, all of whom he insisted he was going to remember in his will.

They all knew that Myles was rich, and it amazed them that he was doing this. He was careful about the wording and that all their names were included and spelled correctly. They were to divide his wealth equally among themselves, with no conditions or favoritism. Doc held the paper, and Orville supported Myles's arm as he feebly signed it. That done, Myles smiled around at all of them. Then he died.

Orville excitedly counted them and himself. "Nine of us! Whatever it is, we got to split it nine ways. But that could still come to quite a lot! How much do you think he was worth, Doc?"

Doc was preoccupied and said nothing. Then he took Raider aside, and Orville saw Raider nodding and laughing vigorously.

Doc turned to them all. "The bank in Coronado where

Myles kept his gold was destroyed in the tornado. Whatever cash the wind didn't take was picked over by looters. Myles had gotten this news. That last will and testament was his final joke on humanity, and that wasn't a friendly smile on his face as he died. He was laughing at us."